AUTOPSY
of a
FATHER

AUTOPSY
of a
FATHER

Pascale Kramer

English translation by Robert Bononno

BELLEVUE LITERARY PRESS
NEW YORK

First published in the United States in 2017 by
Bellevue Literary Press, New York

For information, contact:
Bellevue Literary Press
NYU School of Medicine
550 First Avenue
OBV A612
New York, NY 10016

Autopsy of a Father first appeared in French as *Autopsie d'un père*,
© 2016 by Flammarion

Library of Congress Cataloging-in-Publication Data
is available from the publisher upon request

Bellevue Literary Press would like to thank all its generous
donors—individuals and foundations—for their support.

 This publication is made possible by the New York
State Council on the Arts with the support of Governor
Andrew Cuomo and the New York State Legislature.

 This project is supported in part
by an award from the National
Endowment for the Arts.

With the support of the Swiss Arts Council Pro Helvetia

Book design and composition by Mulberry Tree Press, Inc.

Manufactured in the United States of America.
First Edition

1 3 5 7 9 8 6 4 2

paperback ISBN: 978-1-942658-24-5
ebook ISBN: 978-1-942658-25-2

For Agnès on this sad June 10

AUTOPSY
of a
FATHER

PROLOGUE

THE RETENTION PONDS had just been crossed. The train was now moving over the final patches of tilled earth, raked with copper beneath the low autumn sun. Soon the forest would appear, the tunnels, and the rush of crowded trains along the viaduct, with the seemingly endless expanse of the distant city before it. Gabriel rested his forehead against the glass. Below him, a man in boots had emerged from a path, swaying in the brambles before the onslaught of small stones kicked up from the tracks. There was a long scream, then the man's face, a marked face, half eaten by the hood of his parka, appeared in the gale left by the passing train. Gabriel leaned over to watch him as he disappeared in the distance. A brief vision of solitude that forced him to confront his own.

It made no sense to have left. The silence, the doubt—they wouldn't be any easier to bear in Monceau. It would have been better simply to wait for Clara's return to Les Épinettes. Without her, Gabriel was no longer able to overcome the anxiety of those dark hours before evening, when the garden began to form a single block with the night against the living room windows. He was no longer even certain she would be returning this evening. She hadn't called before leaving, hadn't answered his calls, either at home or on her cell phone. Maybe she was more shaken up than she wanted to admit by what he had been through. Maybe if he had been able to laugh at himself, he thought, having anticipated so little of the isolation of banishment to which he had condemned himself by that single sentence, although one he did not deny having said.

THE WALL STRUCK HIS TEMPLE with the passage of another train. Gabriel straightened up; the glass disappeared in a flutter of gold light as the tracks cut through the forest. He rose from his seat to grab a newspaper left in the luggage rack above him. That's when he saw them, Ania and little Théo, in the first row of seats near the door to the car.

It was hard to believe they hadn't seen one another on the platform, strange too that she had taken the train at this late hour. Gabriel wondered what she had done, who she had gone to see after showing up without warning, wrapped in some kind of bohemian kerchief, her desire for provocation so obvious that he hadn't even noticed it. It wasn't like her to have maintained contact with anyone in the village. Unless she had remained friends with Chloé, he thought, picturing in his mind the features of that slightly soiled child with the very pale eyes, who had come with her mother to a birthday party more than thirty years ago.

With one leg folded beneath him, little Théo daydreamed facing the window. Gabriel watched him press his thumb against the glass as if to arrest the passage of the landscape upon which would be superimposed the oval of his delicate face, cut high and straight by the fringe of hair. The boy hadn't yet noticed that his mother was crying, quick tears that she brushed aside with the tips of her fingers. But he soon tried to get her attention, grazed her wet cheek and turned to wrap her in his arms, with a movement both concerned and painful. Gabriel couldn't get over the maturity of intention and empathy; only a short while ago, he had found the boy to be awkward, timid, and sullen.

Ania let herself be consoled, her torso bent toward the child, her eyes gazing off into space. It was strange to be able to observe his own daughter without her knowledge, and on that very day. Gabriel decided not to reveal his presence; what more could they have to say? Yet he would have liked to know whether she was crying because of him or for him, the scandalous father whose attitude had so scandalized others, or—at least that's what he had told her in the garden to cut short any comments—had offered hypocritical and naïve individuals a moment of cheap unanimity.

THE TRAIN HAD REACHED THE WESTERN SUBURB, an expanse of old buildings a few stories high interspersed with trees reflected in the mirrored surfaces of office towers. In places, a kitchen garden abutted a brick shed or tangled with scrub grass between the piers of the viaduct. From the frontmost car, where Gabriel was seated, the sky seemed within reach; a blimp advanced almost imperceptibly, puncturing a lingering cloud.

The sun, which had fallen along the edge of the tracks, crossed the car from end to end; Théo protected himself by pulling up the collar of his polo shirt. Ania had regained her composure and was telling him something with rapid gestures. They were tossed against one another by the shuddering train. The boy didn't take his eyes off his mother's mouth as he extended a precautionary caress to her still distraught features. What could she be saying to him? Gabriel wondered what kind of picture she was painting of the demanding father whom she had turned against long before adolescence.

With the boy she observed the kind of familiarity found in single mothers, who, out of necessity, had become friends with their children, forced by the problems of adults to mature too quickly. Maybe (probably) she had divorced; in any event, Gabriel wouldn't have known. It had been four years since he had seen her, and there had been nothing that explained or even indicated why. This grandson with such adult concerns must be about six, then. Gabriel had no idea what one understood at that age. He had practically no memory of his own childhood.

THE TRAIN WAS NOW NEARLY FULL, and a crush of passengers attempted to board at every station. Gabriel had forgotten how painful travel could be at this time of day. He had withdrawn against the back of his seat, delaying the moment when he would have to retrieve his bag. Standing near the door to the car, a young man was talking into his phone in some unknown tongue, degraded with

French expletives, while music pulsed from beneath his helmet. A woman, her thighs tightly sheathed in red, had stopped between the seats, waiting with annoyance for a place to free up. Gabriel gathered his things from the seat beside him, without receiving so much as a glance or a thank-you. The woman spread a knit bag of gold chains across her lap from which she pulled the white thread of an earbud. For a second, Gabriel examined her pulpy mouth as it silently voiced a melody, her fake nails, encrusted with spangles, racing over her phone's screen. A strong scent of vanilla reached him like an oily cloud. He turned to the window, pulling on the bottom of his jacket. A wave of almost jubilatory terror rolled over him suddenly. What would they have done, this bunch of ill-mannered riffraff with whom he was now forced to travel, if they had known what he no longer felt any compunction about saying? Would they have strung him up? But these people didn't know anything, didn't know who he was or what he had said, or the words that had gotten him fired. These people didn't read that sort of thing, he said to himself, maybe wouldn't even have understood it. Ultimately, it wasn't so much a question of them as it was of how people saw themselves, how they saw their country. For his part, he felt hopeless as he watched its rigor and intellect slowly seep away.

THE TRAIN WOUND THROUGH THE TUNNELS one by one, accompanied by the noise of switches converging upon the station. It was filled with tired people, by swollen stomachs under wrinkled shirts, by brazen young girls beneath a tangle of red and blue streaks, battalions of the young with downcast eyes, alike in their skin color and their exhaustion, wearing clothes that smelled of spices. Gabriel hated his generation and himself for having allowed that world to impose itself, whether through negligence or idealism. Ania had sought refuge in that confusion, found consolation for her inadequacies there. For a time, she had even attended the mosques and hammams; this was upon her return from a sentimental journey to Iran that had, in the end, been so far from—and so painfully—the country of her mother. That's how he had lost her once and for all. He had felt remorse, yes, and she aggression, and in the end he had simply resigned himself, whatever she might think, to keeping his distance.

Because of the scrum of passengers standing in the aisle of the train, he could no longer see her. When they arrived, Gabriel couldn't find her on the platform either. He imagined her hurrying to catch the express train, the boy trotting by her side, no taller than the zippers, bags, and strollers around him. Unless she had moved, which was certainly possible, it would be at least another hour before she got home, another hour of this unbearable promiscuity among the world's loners. What sort of injury, of which he was supposedly the cause, was she pretending to avenge by this life of mediocrity? He at least could have insisted that she not deprive him of the ability to see the boy. That's what Clara thought, no doubt rightly, and with more conviction than he.

AT THE EXIT OF THE STATION, he was surprised by the night, soft and windswept. He walked down Malesherbes. Rows of chestnut trees shook their reddish leaves, as large as a closed fist. In fifteen minutes he was home, in the small apartment in Monceau he had bought thirty years earlier, when he had started his weekly history broadcast.

His mailbox was overflowing with a hodgepodge of brochures and letters, which he deposited in the entranceway. The fridge was empty. Outside, along the park fence, a man was painstakingly arranging his cardboard and bags for the night. Gabriel had no desire to eat; he was overcome with nausea, nausea and fear. The condemnation to which he had been subjected the past several weeks had led to an uneasiness that fatigue and distance had only made more obvious. He wrote this in his diary. It was a kind of preface, a way to approach the many pages about the sensation of oppression that had made the house feel hostile and his isolation so overwhelming in Clara's absence.

He also alluded to Ania's reappearance, describing the puffy face, almost unrecognizable within the oval of her scarf, the unpleasant shock of finding her, after all this time, on his doorstep, without time to prepare, and her detachment, which had, in spite of everything, managed to affect him.

It was nine when he closed the diary. He had reheated a plate of noodles and served himself a shot of vodka in a mustard jar. Clara's flight had landed on time but she hadn't gotten home yet. He left her a final message to let her know he was in town. Before hanging up, he added that he thought he had seen a man throw himself onto the tracks, a laborer, maybe a railroad employee, a man from the world of hard work that had been that of his parents, a world gone by, discredited, a world for which he would never feel nostalgic.

THE PAPER WAS LYING ON THE TABLE in the small room used by the staff at the day care center. It was open to the programs page, where Gabriel's photo adorned a short article partly covered by some rapid scribbling. It was a fine photo, composed, unspeakably bitter, which Ania remembered quite clearly. It had appeared maybe ten years earlier, when her father's appointment as head of a national radio station had received the support of several newspapers. Ania was then sharing an apartment in a building in Suresnes, and she returned to Les Épinettes rarely, if at all. Gabriel had sent the article—like everything about himself he felt was important—to her home, together with a short note: "Just to let you know. Your father. Kisses." Just to let her know what exactly? she had often wondered. That he was successful? That he was keeping up the connection she was trying to avoid? His letters were proof of a life she had known only superficially: the familiarity with power, the hours of reading, silent and bored, on the deep living room sofas, the Sunday visitors and their condescending informality toward the village. Gabriel didn't expect Ania to speak to him about the articles, nor did he expect that she would be proud of them. He had never been impressed by fame, least of all his own.

Ania turned the paper over and went to prepare some tea and make sure that Lucia, her colleague, was still outside. The precaution was unnecessary, however, for Lucia would never have believed that the man in the photograph was Ania's father, and had little interest in the matter to begin with. She remained there smoking, squatting on her heels, her face buried up to her cheeks in the fake fur collar of a red coat that, at one time, Gabriel would have found amusing.

The previous day, the station had announced that Gabriel was being let go at the request of the entire editorial team. The article didn't discuss the "misstep" that had triggered their unanimity against him; there must have been enough commentary about that already. Ania hadn't heard about it, though. She knew so little about what was going on, really, but could easily imagine just how far her father might have gone.

The photograph framed his face. The mouth, clearly delineated, smiled on one side, his gaze fixed on the lens through the reflections in his glasses. It was the same face, sensual and intelligent, whose irony she had feared and had withdrawn from ever since she was eight. Yet on that day, in the noisy proximity of the children waking from their nap, her inadequacy now seemed inconsequential to her. A handful of beautiful soft garnet blooms were still visible on the low rosebushes planted just outside the playroom windows. Ania had wonderful memories of those early fall days of gentle torpor on the lawn of Les Épinettes, overlooking the broad ribbon of dark water. Théo had seen the photos, and he couldn't understand why they had never been invited. Ania planned to take him the following weekend if the weather held out. Gabriel had always been interested in small children. He had even managed to be a comforting father for the first few years, when the two of them had been alone.

STEPPING IN THE TALL GRASS by the side of the road, along the stretch of land that separated the train station from Les Épinettes, and keeping a careful eye on Théo as he walked lopsidedly in his sneakers, Ania realized that Gabriel might not be home, or not alone. She remembered now that it had been four years since they had spoken. At least she could have found out why he had been let go from the station. Much against her will, the old anxiety about her ignorance returned to life as she approached the house.

The road leading to the entrance of the property was still deeply furrowed and covered with polished stones half buried in the dirt. The gate was wide open as always; Ania didn't know how to explain to Théo Gabriel's habit of never closing doors. The untrimmed ivy overflowed the garden wall like a bundle of laundry, and the tall lime trees, encrusted with mistletoe, now joined together above the shed where the tools and bicycles were stored. The old Audi that Gabriel used to get around the village was still there, parked in the same spot in the shadows of the branches.

It took him a long time to respond, even though the music had stopped when she first rang the bell. Their presence surprised him less than it disturbed him, although he tried to conceal it. His face had grown thinner beneath the sheen of white hair, which he had worn short for the past few years. His eyes, riddled with small capillaries, took pleasure in observing how she had changed, especially the weight she had put on, which he was careful not to mention. He then turned to Théo, looked at him fixedly for a long time, as if he were trying to find in him the small boy he had seen here four years earlier. "You've come at a bad time," he said at last, indulging Ania with a smile. "After all these years, you could have let me know in advance, don't you think?" Ania told him that she had decided on the spur of the moment, after seeing his picture in the paper. Gabriel responded to her frankness with an ironic arching of his eyebrows. He asked them to

Autopsy of a Father

wait five minutes; they could sit outside, the chairs were already out.

Théo had made a great deal of this visit to his grandfather. The welcome and wildness of the large garden left him feverish. He had released his mother's hand, suddenly behaving as if others were observing him. Ania rediscovered the place through his eyes, which were now accustomed to the anarchy of the suburbs. The cherry trees were beginning to cloak themselves with red. The ropes of the swing, left to rot for years on end, were gone. In front of the house, the wicker chairs had, in fact, been placed on the grass. They'd been painted white. At the bottom of the garden, she noticed a reed lattice screening one of the buildings of the neighboring property: a pretty structure with a flat roof whose doors and shutters Ania had always seen closed. Several large clusters of hydrangea were in bloom.

"IF YOU'RE HERE ABOUT WHAT HAPPENED," Gabriel said, rejoining them with a pitcher of cold verbena and some leftover ice cream for Théo, "I'll tell you right away that I'm not interested in your opinion." His sly, bitter eyes held her own. Ania would have liked to tell him that his little games no longer had any effect on her. But he wouldn't have understood; he would have furrowed his brow at the word "games" as he painfully tried to follow her, as he did when she was a girl, listening to her hesitant and always poorly formulated replies. So she sat back in her chair facing the sun and let him talk, listening with half an ear. He made no attempt to find out what she had been doing, what had become of her. It had been like that ever since she'd left home. He asked nothing, as if to indicate that he was complying with her desire to live her life differently somewhere else. On the other hand, he was talkative when it came to himself, answering questions she did not ask about his plans for the apartment in Monceau, now that he had lost the few bylines that remained to him, and the caretakers' house here, since they would be retiring in three or four years.

Théo finished his ice cream without taking his

eyes off his grandfather in his T-shirt, who spoke in long sentences, massaging the wicker armrests with his delicate hands. He had no experience, not even any notion, of these distant and cultivated environments in which Ania had felt so ill at ease as a child. She sensed this in his combination of fascination and discomfort, hesitant whether to sit and watch or go off exploring.

Behind the row of poplars that Gabriel had had planted to protect himself from the hordes of weekend kayakers, the river's heavy waters tossed bits of wood around as the light flickered gently across the surface. Théo had finally worked up the courage to advance to the bottom of the lawn, where he discovered the small gate, now covered with briars and nettles and indistinguishable from the fence itself. Ania saw him step carefully among the thorns as he drew closer. He would soon turn around to reassure himself she had seen him and was allowing him to go as far as the river. Gabriel suddenly grew quiet and leaned forward in his chair to follow the boy with his eyes. "Don't try to open it. And make sure you don't enter the neigh-bors' property," he shouted, and then again, louder this time. So, he had even forgotten that Théo couldn't hear; it was astounding he could forget something like that. Ania was stunned, her ears buzzed. She grabbed her bag, put on her shoes, and glared at her father as if he were someone she might have had difficulty remembering.

"You know I sold the last Degas, I had expenses from the house," he announced, extending his arm in the direction of the library, where the drawing had been hanging for years. Théo was returning from his exploration of the garden, small, green prickly berries clinging to his socks. Gabriel drew back to observe him fully, as if honoring him with this more serious interest. "Next time, tell your mother to let me know at least an hour ahead of time, then we can take a ride in the Zodiac," he suggested before escorting them to the gate. Along the way he pointed out a cluster of peonies planted the previous year that had already bloomed abun-dantly that spring, and, in the blackened hollow of an oak, the remains of a hornets' nest he had had to burn away.

There was a photo of her at the age of four, running behind him across the scorched lawn, red with poppies, which sloped down to the glassy surface of the water. It was a time when Gabriel wanted no one but her in his retirement as a widower, seeing his friends only after she had gone to bed, and rarely women, whose presence Ania knew of only through the hushed conversations in the hallway, the footsteps on the stairs, the brief flash of headlights in the early-morning haze beneath the trees.

"You remember how we could see the river from here?" he said, laughing pointlessly at this allusion to happier times. He even moved closer to kiss her, saying, "Finally, with your permission," in that seductive tone he had adopted with her ever since she had ceased to be pretty. Théo stood a few steps away with a kind of timid resistance. He took hold of the hand that Gabriel extended to him with some seriousness. His small face shaped itself into a frown. Ania could see that it was she he was angry with, angry for the fact that they were practically being thrown out.

Gabriel didn't wait till they were at the gate to utter a final goodbye and close himself in. Ania sought Théo's hand in the hope that he would now see her side of things. But his stubbornness persisted, and he protested that they should have told him they were coming, as Gabriel had said. His reaction annoyed her. "Your grandfather doesn't even remember that you can't hear," she blurted out, as she turned aside with bitterness. Théo pulled her by the sleeve so she would stop. He wanted to know what she had said, and the fact that she might not want to repeat it made him tremble. His ill humor had drained away but not his anger or his disappointment. Ania could have cried for what she had put him through.

It was still early, too early to return home. Ania suggested they go down to the river, where they could walk past the neighboring properties along a narrow strip of well-worn earth, cluttered with thorn bushes and convolvulus, against which clumps of foam-flecked seaweed lapped. She remembered a small pebble-covered beach, a tiny cove in a field of grazing sheep. Her mother used to bring her there to swim even though the current was strong and the area infested with horseflies that hurled themselves against her like projectiles. It was one of the rare images Ania retained of her mother: her broad, garnet-colored smile, her face emerging, disheveled, from the tight-fitting dresses she drew off like a stocking, as she shouted encouragement and ran toward the water. The summer following her death, Gabriel had come there several times with Ania, as if something of her mother remained that would bring the illusion back to life. He would wait for her to enter the water, then follow her on foot along the path all the way to the floating pier, a few hundred meters below, from which she could climb back up to the bank. The hint of danger he caused her to experience was part of the wonderful complicity from which she had drawn, even as a little girl, a feeling of completion.

THERE WERE NO MORE SHEEP; the entrance to the field had been blocked by barbed wire that Théo was unable to navigate. He looked around, annoyed and put off by the odor of mud and the incessant swarm of flies that vibrated near him. Ania decided to return home but walked along the back road this time to avoid passing in front of Les Épinettes. And it was when she recognized the low house off in the distance and below the roadway that she decided to visit Chloé. She was curious to again experience the unimaginable disorder of a family in which, as an adolescent, she had felt sheltered and could retaliate against the distasteful world of her father.

Chloé didn't appear surprised to see them. She hadn't changed, small and round, with the look of a different time, her soft, freckled skin framed by the brilliant curls of her jet-black hair, swept back from her face. Théo was reluctant to kiss her or even enter the house, offended by the disorder of the garden where, beneath the undisciplined luxuriance of the fruit trees and untrimmed hedges, had been amassed a jumble of chairs, wooden boards, empty bottles, bicycle wheels, and broken toys, in which colonies of centipedes and earwigs burrowed. Ania let go of his hand, allowing him to deal with his cowardice by himself.

Chloé watched as he looked for a place to sit beneath the arbor of shriveled berries that stained the chairs and concrete black. "You're deaf," she said, waiting until their eyes met. Ania had always known her to be like this (and envied her for it): strange and cruel, impervious to criticism, ignorant too but with implacable self-assurance. She didn't give Théo the time to reply, to assume the painful timbre of his strange, artificial voice in front of this unconventional young woman. That he might have suspected that she was suddenly ashamed of him made her miserable.

BACK WHEN THEY WERE IN THE SAME CLASS in the village, Chloé was living alone with her obese mother, a woman who slept through the day surrounded by yellow and black canaries, feverishly alert amid the stench of bird shit, feed, and lard. One of the cages, its door torn off, had been placed beneath the arbor. "The best were sold," Chloé said, in response to Théo's intrigued glance at the empty cage, now filled with faded advertising brochures.

A baby had begun to cry from behind a shutter looking out onto the terrace. Chloé took her time responding and soon returned with a chubby little girl a few months old still flushed with sleep. Ania knew that the three oldest children had been placed and was surprised that Chloé hadn't mentioned it yet. She felt guilty for having dragged Théo into this slightly sordid chaos. Seated, hunched over, he waited for the opportunity to leave. Ania couldn't get him to look at her.

"We saw your father in the paper and on the news recently," Chloé told her after she brought the child back inside. "You don't live here any longer, but I know that he's right about what's going on; the idiot neighbors can say what they want." Her tone was rational, proud. Ania made no attempt to pursue the matter. It wasn't impossible that Gabriel had finally found himself in agreement with people like Chloé in rejecting the dusky world that would soon be at their doorstep. She felt sick to her stomach, a kind of deep melancholy. Théo was still hunched over, scraping the crushed grape seeds with the tips of his sneakers. They would have to wait more than an hour on the platform, but Ania didn't think she could remain any longer. While walking them to the road, Chloé found a dirt-covered figurine in the grass that she handed to Théo. He tossed it into the branches of a cherry tree as soon as the gate closed behind them.

When they reached the train station, the boy had a tantrum that Ania was unable to account for and that deeply disturbed her. It was the way he grew angry when Novak forced him to spar and in his zeal often knocked him over. Although his affection for the boy's fragile clumsiness was sincere, Théo fought back with an energetic and tearful fury.

THÉO RUSHED TO THE PHONE as soon as it started blinking. Ania watched him disappear, limping into the blue shadow of morning inside the apartment. His frailty and nervousness surprised her suddenly as she observed his bare thighs and little boy's underwear. He was much calmer since Novak was no longer living there and the school had provided them with a routine, but he always seemed to be anxiously waiting for something that Ania could only hope to discover.

"Here," he said, holding the phone at the end of his arm. His head was covered with unruly tufts of hair that Ania smoothed with her hand, making a sign for him to take a shower and get dressed. The click of a lighter could be heard on the phone, then a very self-assured and feminine "Hello." Ania felt her heart skip a beat. It had to be Clara.

"You know who I am, don't you?" Clara said after that brief introduction. "Your father died last night in his apartment in Monceau," she continued, with almost no change in her youthful, firm, and pleasant voice. "He swallowed some glass, nine pieces, fairly large, from a mustard jar," she added, exhaling the smoke of her cigarette just as she would have sneered at the unbearable idea of repeatedly swallowing a razor. "He died from internal bleeding, probably during the evening; his body was already starting to smell when I got there from the airport this morning, it must have been around six." Clara appeared to sniffle angrily as she reported this detail. Ania remained silent, more fascinated by the voice than the news. Her mind resisted the idea that he had died at Monceau when she had just seen him the day before, indolent and derisive, at Les Épinettes, his world.

Most likely, Clara was calling from her car and probably returning to the apartment. She suggested to Ania that they meet there. She said this with the same strangely distinct voice, leaving no room for questions and as if they had agreed there would be no tears. The news, at that early hour on a gloomy Sunday morning, gave them a sense of immediate familiarity. "Gabriel and I had made a marriage contract, so you'll get everything that's yours," Clara added, before asking if it were possible to meet around three.

Ania didn't know about the marriage. She had the impression of having been rapidly swept up in events that she should have known from the first. To establish not a distance but her own rhythm, she asked Clara to repeat the address, and explained that she would try to stop by but made no promises. Ania was barely five when Gabriel purchased the small two-room apartment. She had slept there a few times back then, remembering it as an airless place where her father became someone she didn't know. She never imagined she would one day have to immerse herself in that world again.

IT WAS NEARLY TEN O'CLOCK. Behind the closed blinds, the day—a Sunday, October 3—was beginning, a day to be remembered. Gabriel would have been fifty-eight years old in a month, she reminded herself, placing the phone back in its cradle in the living room. No new memory would replace that of his erect torso and his tender voice calling out to Théo, who had gone to explore the thick border of nettles surrounding the property. What kind of despair could have led to the death of a man capable of forgetting his own family?

Théo had turned on the television; he still wasn't dressed. Sitting on the floor at the height of the low table, he carefully separated and arranged the pieces of a puzzle one by one. His thin legs ended in a coil of socks. Beneath the pajama top, now too short, peeked the small sharp bones of his spine. Ania turned the ceiling light on and off to let him know she was there, but Théo didn't lift his head. Nor did he ask who had called. Ania didn't know how you told a child about his grandfather's death. She decided there was no urgency in doing so, nor any obligation, for that matter. Seeing him seated on the rug, sulking and painstakingly removing the pieces of the puzzle and putting them in their box, Ania guessed that something more profound than mere disappointment had taken place the day before. He appeared to be angry with her for failing to win her father's approval while they were at Les Épinettes; he may even have felt her to be responsible for what had happened. A feeling of profound unfairness arose in her like a bitter liquid. She saw Gabriel, sitting sideways in the wicker armchair, describing his plans to make use of the freedom he would now enjoy, displaying his satisfaction at the scandal he had caused, and amused by her own opinion of it. She thought it was madness that he was so evasive and yet so fully at ease.

Ania had withdrawn to her bedroom, closing the door to have a little privacy. From the living room came the noise of the puzzle pieces that Théo was shaking around in the box. She turned on the radio, slowly scanning the dial until she came upon the familiar voices of her childhood.

Gabriel had always worked with a radio playing softly. The sound of the programs hadn't changed, it was that of the studious silence of Les Épinettes, the sound of boredom. Ania shut it off to slow the progress of the past in her. Besides, the news was over, and it was highly unlikely that reports of his death had begun to circulate. She tried to reach Novak, then his roommate these past few years in Suresnes, but didn't leave a message. Something else suddenly began to bother her—what Gabriel had said about the Degas.

There had been three of them, ocher-colored pastel drawings of female nudes in contorted postures. They were part of his inheritance from his mother, and they had always hung opposite the bed in the upstairs bedroom. That was all Ania knew when this one, the most muted of the three, had been brought down to the library. Why had her father sold the other two, and when? Ania had never concerned herself with his financial situation. In her childhood imagination, the relative wealth that had allowed her mother and them to lead a life of elegant bohemianism was an immutable fact. Part of that inheritance—the collection of paintings and drawings, at least—had come directly to her, she was almost certain. An appraisal had, in fact, been made; she could see where the drawings had hung on the bedroom wall. If there were any documents from that time, they had to be at Les Épinettes. But after boarding school, Ania had gone directly to Suresnes, without ever bothering to clear out her childhood bedroom.

The television was off and Théo's spindly silhouette soon appeared in the open doorway. He still hadn't washed or dressed and, as if he were sickened by the thought that he no longer knew where she was, Ania teased him, telling him how odd he looked in his abbreviated pajama top and bare, blue-veined thighs. But Théo wanted to know what she was doing in the bedroom. He couldn't bear the fact that she might be hiding her feelings. And because she refused to answer him, he pressed her cheeks with his fists to force her to open her mouth. Ania pulled back, complaining that he was hurting her. The boy frowned. Beneath the fringe of hair, his eyes examined her angrily. She held his chin and made him look at her.

"Your grandfather had an accident," she slowly articulated. "He died last night." Théo suddenly turned beet red. He remained standing before her, his face turned aside. Ania was angry with herself for having put him, without warning, in a situation to which he didn't know how to respond. She ran her finger across his forehead as she often did to ease his vulnerability. "It's not all that bad, you know, we hardly ever saw him." Théo agreed, gravely, still red and frowning. Ania bent over him to hike up his socks. "I have to go out this afternoon; is there a friend you could stay with?" Théo listened, his chin sunk into the collar of his pajama. He wanted to go with her or stay by himself. That she insisted that he visit a friend made him stamp his feet with rage, like the day before at the train station when she had finally grown angry. Ania told herself she should never have brought him to see his grandfather.

She did get the name of a friend, Augustin, whose mother showed herself to be both concerned and efficient, volunteering to drive over and take her to the train station. Théo took a long time to decide what to wear and what to bring with him. His agitation was real, though; Ania knew that, because of her, his lack of experience was complete, as was his wariness of others.

THE CAR STOPPED AT THE END OF THE STREET and blinked its lights. Augustin's mother had had difficulty finding the house and her nearly juvenile face retained a slight sign of impatience that contradicted the extreme warmth of her welcome. She moved the seat back for Ania, excusing the mess of crumpled papers she told her to ignore, then turned to Théo with a serious smile. At once the two boys began to talk; Ania found that Théo's gestures were more demonstrative than customary.

He seemed to be relaxed with them, but she worried that he wouldn't know how to behave or feel comfortable in their presence. She so rarely entrusted him to others that she saw everything as threatening for the boy.

The mother drove quickly and barefoot, her red high heels stored beneath the seat. She'd turned the radio on, asking if it would bother Ania, as if music could affect her sorrow. Her son was preoccupied with a video game. He was wearing some sort of patch on his head and thick glasses behind which his face appeared very distant. Ania admired the fact that someone could be so lively and attractive even with a child with his disabilities.

The car arrived at the train station. Théo had climbed between the seats, and Ania could hear the sighs of his growing depression buzzing in her ear. She would have liked to leave without too much fuss, but Théo insisted on getting out of the car to kiss her. His tears, which he had held back until then, began to flow, and Ania could feel their damp warmth against her stomach. She lifted his face, which stuttered with anger because Augustin had seen this display of emotion. But the boy paid no attention; his mother had taken him to pick out some magazines. Ania found her to be thoughtful and easygoing, and felt she had betrayed the woman's sympathy.

CLARA HADN'T CLOSED THE DOOR behind her on the landing. Ania knocked, then pushed it open. She was surprised by the stale odor of soiled linens and aging skin that the fresh air did little to improve. A sheet from a notebook slipped between her feet as the door shut behind her. Ania had no memory of the place, more like an impression that she could not fully recall, something akin to a young girl's intuition that her father was someone else. The window at the end of the hallway was open; Ania discovered the view into the park—a thick blanket of red-marbled leaves like a coat.

Clara was in the bedroom; she shouted that she would be right there. Ania hung her bag in the entrance hall, adjusted her ponytail, regretting that she hadn't bothered to make herself look more attractive for their first meeting. Behind her, the bathroom door was ajar. Ania remembered her disgust as a child with having to place her bare feet on the tile floor. She pushed the door and turned on the bare bulb, which cast reflections off the dark green tile. Towels were strewn around the bathtub. A plastic razor encrusted with dirty shaving cream lay on the edge of the sink together with a pharmacy's worth of medications of a man eager to die. Ania felt the intimacy of a father whom she had known only by his behavior; it was both painless and embarrassing.

The office also looked out onto the park. It was filled, on two sides, with piles of erudite books and newspapers. A large photo of a woman faced the door from within a jumble of paintings and thumb-tacked pages. The face was cut off just above the mouth, the arms rounded into a bow, as if cradling the small, naked breasts redefined by the contrast of black and white in the extension of the hollow musculature of her stomach. Ania was pleased to note that the photo hadn't replaced that of her parents, whose memory now returned with a heartfelt pang. The photograph wore the colors of summer and was taken shortly before their marriage, among her mother's own family, near Tehran.

Clara had just entered the room, her hands on her hips in a kind of haughty and friendly naturalness. She bent toward the picture of the couple sitting in the wind on a beach at nightfall. "They were married so young," she said, holding out a supple hand on which Ania recognized the diamond in the black-and-white portrait, a small stone set atop a fragile ring, as fine as a hair.

She was a beautiful woman, with an uncustomary, almost martial, beauty, and younger than Ania had imagined—she must have been no more than a few years older than she was, thirty-eight or so—yet she wasn't a young woman, being too sure of herself and conventional. She revealed nothing of what she had gone through that morning. To her great surprise, Ania felt somewhat moved by their introduction. "We could have hoped for more pleasant circumstances," Clara joked, before adding, "maybe you'd like me to show you . . ." with the same pragmatism she had displayed on the phone. Ania followed her to the bedroom, where the drawn shutters burned with fine streaks of light. So this is where it happened, she thought, without managing to convince herself.

The mattress had been removed. Beneath the bare slats of the bed were two drops of blood, a shiny seal on the film of dust that covered the disorderly pages and used tissues. "There are companies that do only that, remove blood-soaked mattresses," Clara said, taking a cigarette from a package. "At least I'll have learned something." With a broad movement of her torso, she indicated the exact position of the body, fully clothed on the bed, the face a few inches from the wall, then turned in the direction of the desk, where she had found the remains of the broken glass. "First he tried to cut his wrists," she said, leaning against the wall. Her voice broke from time to time. Ania remembered that she had said she had arrived at the airport only that morning; she probably hadn't slept. Her strange familiarity with the violence of the facts spared Ania from having to make pretenses or provide justifications.

"I didn't touch his journal." Clara pointed to an orange notebook placed alongside a small aerosol can on the shelf by the bed. "I'll leave you to look at it," she said as she left the room. Ania listened to her steps fade along the floorboards; Clara's concern for Ania gave her the first real sign of emotion since that morning.

The notebook was sticky with syrup. Ania didn't know whether it was from fear or the desire that he might have written about their last meeting that she decided to open it. She was there, in fact, a few pages from the end, in tears and being consoled by Théo in the train. Ania closed the notebook and put it down. Her body burned with the humiliation of letting herself be surprised by him while she was crying. She looked at the aerosol can, the old tissues, and the small red splotches in the dust beneath the bed, seeking in vain to connect them with her confusion.

CLARA WAS WAITING IN FRONT of the office window, one hand placed on her neck as if to keep her head from falling. She had been hoping for something from the notebook, an explanation, yet asked no questions. Imperceptibly, the distress began to overtake the courage she had displayed. Ania admired the fact that one could remain so composed under the circumstances. Where had she arrived from early that morning? It hadn't entered Ania's mind before that they might have had an argument or separated in such a way that Clara felt herself to be responsible.

Clara had prepared a draft of the notice of death, which she handed her. Ania read: *His daughter, Ania Delâcre-Janic, his grandson Théo, his son-in-law Novak Janic*, and remained silent, stunned. She would never have dreamed of an announcement. Now she would have to decide whether to put her name on it or not, and either way, the decision seemed wrong to her. "You think that's what he would have wanted?" she asked, handing back the piece of paper. Clara remarked that now they wouldn't have to worry about it. Her irritability reflected a kind of bitter anger toward Gabriel. For Clara was angry with him, Ania began to understand, and her actions grew harsher in having to defend herself against the unjust brutality of what he had forced her to endure. Against the light her face was marked by deep shadows. Her bones were visible beneath the skin, and the broad outline of her jaw contrasted with the long, slender bust, tightly wrapped in a light-colored fabric. She must have learned to never feel pity for herself, Ania thought, smiling, there's something ecclesiastic about her.

The air began to grow cool and the sun withdrew from the rooms. Clara went over to look at his laptop, which sat on the desk, and then turned back to Ania. "Gabriel told me you didn't know how to read," she said, staring at her with a kind of attentive and strangely warmhearted objectivity. Ania raised her eyebrows, amazed at the lack of concern her father had had for others in creating his legend. "And you thought it was true?" she replied. Clara smiled but in fact was no longer listening. She was exhausted, and probably hadn't showered, and the slightly sour odor from her armpits established an intimacy between them that was only slightly out of place. Ania suspected in her that special calm found in those who remain untouched by the judgments of others. Clara had married Gabriel even though his name had already begun to give off the stench of defeat. Ania was unable to imagine her giving in, as he had these past few years, to a revulsion for the world he lived in, or she must have done so with much more distance and serenity.

Clara had brought over an armchair for Ania and sat down beneath the open window, asking if she minded that she smoked. From the sidewalk, the sound of a container being brought back into the building could be heard. The russet of the trees occupied nearly the entire window. For a moment, Clara allowed herself to be hypnotized by the waves stirred by the wind. "Did you come here often?" she asked Ania, waving the smoke out the window. "Once or twice at most, the year he bought it." At that moment the impression began to take shape that she had become a burden for the first time in her father's life. The couple they formed and that Gabriel adored, the widower and the little girl, needed Les Épinettes, the garden that sloped down nearly to the water beneath the centenarian trees, and the house, of which they occupied hardly more than the barn-like living room, leaving him to its nooks and crannies and the rooms beneath the roof. Ania tried to formulate that tenuous impression, which Clara appeared to understand. At least, she maintained her concentration before making a slow sign of acquiescence, a belated reaction to what she had just heard. "I was never very welcome here myself. Among other things because that forced him to clean the place up," she said with a trembling smile crossed by a tear. Her anger gave way. She stared at the glowing tip of her cigarette, seeming to slowly let what had happened sink in. Ania had the impression of touching her suffering with her finger. "Did my father tell you why I stopped coming?" Clara smiled oddly. "I don't think he knew why." She made a gesture with her hand, as if to sweep away any unpleasant reasons he may have considered. A silence followed into which burst the furious barking of two dogs lunging at one another through the park gates. Clara stood up to close the window. She pointed to another laptop, on the floor, near piles of books that had fallen, informing her that she had deleted all his accounts and profiles. Ania could very well imagine the types of comments that must have accumulated recently and didn't inquire further. Her father's provocations no longer worked when seen from the slightly tawdry surroundings of a bitter man. Ania was even surprised that they had been taken so seriously. Death doesn't help you much, she mused. Gabriel must not have planned his own, he would have done a better job of staging it. It would be left to Clara to throw away the medications, the old razors, the soiled towels, the sickening writings. What would she retain of his presence in her eyes after all this? Unless she had loved him with a tenderness that had been truly exceptional.

Looking out across the park, Clara remained in

her own world, her lips pressed together. A wooden barrette held the knot of straight, light auburn hair, which coiled across her cheek like soft down. She has no color, Ania realized. No makeup other than the simple beauty of intelligence and a good education, something intimidating, virile in a way, which must have deeply affected her father.

He had spoken of her only once, Ania remembered it perfectly: that she wrote magnificent letters. That was a few years ago. She had spent a Saturday at Les Épinettes. Théo had just turned two, and Gabriel had insisted on inviting them, he had something he wanted to give them. They had barely arrived when he pointed with his finger at a long coat of light-colored leather hanging in the entranceway, saying that there was a woman in his life now, that her name was Clara, and that she wrote magnificent letters. Ania had almost walked out then, for the comment seemed so intentionally cruel.

Her childhood had ended when she began to have trouble at school. Gabriel had interpreted her inability to learn as a form of obstinacy that hurt him and, in so doing, had prevented her, once and for all, from understanding. She had spent her early years in school with her head filled with distractions, withdrawn, as if she lived inside a bell that protected her from his disappointment. With the years, his impatience had ceased to paralyze her. But hearing him talk about that woman's magnificent letters, she knew that no compassion would be forthcoming. She had waited until the end of lunch and the promised gift (of money) to leave, unaware that she would never come back. Yet on that day, Gabriel spoke of nothing other than his infatuation for this woman. He was over fifty; it was the first time since he'd become a widower that he had grown close to anyone. Ania never considered the question of his solitude. Now, she merely evaluated what it might have meant for a womanizer like him, at his age, to be involved physically with this stoic and reserved patrician.

"You went to see him yesterday at Les Épinettes," Clara said, adding, "Might I ask why?" She leaned

forward to crush her cigarette on the stone sill and
sat back against the embrasure, her arms crossed,
without impatience. Ania stared at her, trying
to understand what she wanted to hear. "I know
because he left several messages," Clara answered in
reply to Ania's astonishment. "He didn't say anything else about your visit, but I thought it might
have something to do with this whole idiotic affair."
She took a deep gulp of air, as if she had been holding her breath for a long time. Ania tried to give her
the most honest reason possible, and the following
came to her immediately: she had wanted to show
him that she was less interested in other people's
opinions than he assumed.

Clara listened as she slowly smoothed the leather
on her boots. A faint smile creased her cheek with
a dimple. "He must have seen it otherwise, you
realize that, don't you?" she noted, looking at her
with her handsome, tired face. "He felt demoral-
ized around just about everyone." Ania hesitated a
few seconds before acknowledging that she knew
nothing of the situation other than that they didn't

want him on the radio anymore. The shock must have been considerable, for Clara drew back in a movement of surprise, completely without irony but, rather, with slight admiration. After scrutinizing her for a few moments as if to penetrate her singularity, she rummaged around in the mess beneath the desk and handed her a local newspaper folded just below a large photo of Gabriel taken in front of the city hall of V. A sentence was written in large characters: "I care less about this man's death than the fate of the two young men who grew up here." Clara had taken out a cigarette and lit it after opening the window again. Ania spread the paper across her lap and understood at once upon seeing, farther down in the article, the photograph of a squad of police in the shrubbery.

It was approximately one month since an immigrant from the Comoros had been beaten and drowned by two young men from the region. Ania had heard something about it on the news but had been even more shocked by the fact that because she knew the area, she could imagine the incongruity of

a black man crossing that expanse of rutted countryside in the middle of the night. He was carry-
ing a plastic bag with a container of dried fruit, an
empty wallet, and a ticket for an emergency shelter,
by which one might have assumed that he had been
walking all day long. Three young men from the village had seen him as they were returning from V. on
their scooters, but only two of them had decided to
turn back and grab him. The man walked with long
strides as the empty bag and dark tunic embroidered
with arabesques slapped against him. He began to
walk faster when he heard the scooter coming back,
then headed off into the fields. The two young men
had caught up with him and stabbed him in the
back with a metal picket torn from the dirt. The
body, struck several times, had then been rolled to
the river's edge. They had to hold his face beneath
the stagnant green water by the riverbank until he
was still. It was later discovered that they didn't even
have the excuse of being drunk.

Ania again observed her father's expression in
the photo and that of the closed faces immediately

behind him, then folded the paper. He had taken the side of the murderers; his ideas had gotten that far out of hand. Sincere, as well, since they had, in a way, killed him.

Clara took the newspaper and threw it back where she had found it under the desk. Her feelings about the affair were impossible to discern, and Ania had neither the desire nor the heartlessness to question her. Clara had pulled out a cigarette, which she played with distractedly between her fingers. Her self-assurance appeared to crumble little by little beneath the enveloping weight of her fatigue. There's no place for her to lie down after I'm gone, Ania thought, imagining the small torture she must have experienced in maintaining her composure. What kind of love for a man who had fallen to such extremes enabled her to hold up during moments like these? Ania would have liked to have been more talkative, warmer, but her attention had been distracted by the collection of pictures and photographs in which she was surprised to see herself, two of them especially. One, a small oil, rapidly executed, painted, she thought she recalled, by a rather well-known artist, in which she is shown sitting on her mother's lap. And in a framed photograph of her alone at twelve years of age, seated in the crook of a tree, her legs folded between her arms and her head resting on her knees. The reflections of the leaves dappled her impenetrable features. Ania clearly remembered the day the picture had been taken and who had taken it, but she had never seen it before. It came back to her now, the atmosphere that poisoned her heart that summer, the last one before she left for boarding school.

Her father had invited Mourad, her mother's cousin, for the weekend, a man in exile, a professor without a job, without money, without existence. The man seemed old to her; he was small, with a kind of outmoded elegance, and spoke softly in a feminine voice. At the end of the meal, long after Ania had left the table, he went into the garden and caught sight of her in the tree. He stood there a few moments watching her from below. Ania saw the brilliance of his scalp beneath the thinning hair, carefully parted. Then he came back a little later with a camera, which he slowly raised, as he would have cocked a rifle. Ania didn't protest, didn't move or smile. Her impassiveness before the lens betrayed none of the misery that kept her there. She didn't come back down for a long time after the photograph, enjoying the strange new pleasure of discovering that she was special.

Gabriel himself wasn't in a very good mood that summer either. He had had health problems, which had left him without a sense of smell. The radio program he had been doing for more than two years was probably not going to be picked up in the fall, or it would be moved to a time slot with a smaller audience. The rejection had left him cynical and sardonic, derisive. He had written in an article, the first that Ania had received from him while in boarding school, that, given the growing mediocrity, there was something to be thankful for, in the end, to have been moved to a nighttime slot. The recently republished photograph of him, with that slightly tremulous half smile, had been taken at the time. The insecurity Ania felt in the presence of that smile dampened her spirit. One day, when he had repeated, several times and with that same expression, a word she had mispronounced, she understood that she could never love him again.

"Did he say anything to you about this picture?" Clara moved closer to get a better look. A strand of hair had slipped down her temple. She undid the barrette, which she pinched between her lips so she could redo her hair, gazing at the picture with all the gravity the question required, one whose response was simply that Gabriel had never said anything about it. "Was it during the summer that you had stopped talking to him?" she ventured. Ania rose, preferring to say nothing and especially wishing to learn nothing more about the way her father had described their past. Suddenly, the nervous fatigue of the day and this meeting seemed to exhaust her.

"I'VE DECIDED TO BRING THE BODY back to Les Épinettes," Clara said, as if she had only then remembered, as she walked with Ania down the hallway. "The burial is planned for Saturday." She lifted an eyebrow as if she were defensively awaiting an objection. Ania couldn't get over it and was quite pleased with the woman's efficiency and competence. In fact, she had the impression of being immersed in someone else's grief. Clara asked her if she wouldn't like to take something as a keepsake, the photograph or something else. Ania told her she didn't want anything, only remembering after she had left the building that Théo would have liked the laptop. She realized that Clara must have read Gabriel's journal by now and might have learned something, and was surprised at having so little curiosity, or doubt, about the reasons for her father's actions.

Augustin's mother had left a message to let her know that Théo could spend the night with them if need be. Ania hesitated to call her back. She thought she heard the sound of table soccer in the background but was too much on edge to realize without a certain discomfort that Théo was willing to stay. Without really knowing why, she dialed the number for Les Épinettes. The ringing continued, Ania could hear the ringtone resounding in the open space of the living room. She was again overcome by the apprehension that had strangled her whenever she had had to discuss her vacation. Then someone picked up. It was Jean-Louis. "So you know, then?" he asked soberly, after getting over his surprise. Ania hadn't expected to hear his voice. She said she had seen Clara and would be there for sure the following day if she could find someone to watch Théo. She had decided to find out about the Degas and all the rest.

J EAN-LOUIS HAD COME TO MEET HER. He was
standing in his boots, somewhat off to the side
of the platform darkened by the afternoon rains,
his neck straight and clean shaven beneath the collar of his parka. Ania found that he hadn't aged
much but was slow, almost reticent, in recognizing
her. His face, serious like that of a teacher, still held
the shock of the news. Ania had prepared herself
for this, for finding him deeply affected. But seeing her under these circumstances probably hurt
him more than it otherwise would have. Never-
theless, he allowed himself a modest embrace in
which their bodies met.

He had come in Gabriel's Audi. Ania was surprised to discover, on the folded rear bench, several
bags of soil and fertilizer. "Your father gave it to

us," Jean-Louis explained, seeing her turn around on her seat; "he borrowed it from us those few times he had to go shopping." The conversation stopped then, as if those few words were enough to dry up what remained of his saliva. From time to time, Ania saw him wipe the corner of his eyes with his creviced fingers, the tips of three of which were missing from his right hand. He and his wife, Jacqueline, had moved to Les Épinettes as caretakers shortly after Ania was born. They had stayed there ever since, unmovable and utilitarian, even though Gabriel was soon unable to pay their salary, turning on the heat in winter, killing the wasps and hornets, painting the shutters, scything the grass, raking the leaves. He worked for the maintenance department of the commune of V., and she cleaned house in several of the other large properties along the river. They'd been with him for more than thirty years, which was one of the rare things that Gabriel took seriously and was able to acknowledge. No intimacy had developed between them, only a bond of respectful filiation in which he was a kind of son who had surpassed them in age and understanding. They were the sort of people who went to church, avoided gossip, had a house built in the South for their retirement, and regularly visited the grave of a child who had died after only a few months and whose photograph Ania knew that Jacqueline always kept with her. The idea of suicide must have bothered them more even than the death itself. Indeed, Jean-Louis refused to believe it, as Ania understood from a remark he had made, which she chose to ignore. He preferred silence, which had never been a problem between them; they had always had difficulty understanding each other.

With evening, the sky had cleared. It darkened slowly, vast and pale above the outline of the woods into which the roads disappeared. A banner announcing a weekend flea market flapped between two balconies at the station's exit. A truckload of metal barriers wound with red and white plastic lay on the tilled earth of the traffic circle. Ania told herself that the stall locations would have already been marked in chalk on the sidewalk; she was surprised that the memory of these things came back to her so easily.

A BLACK MINI, WHICH MUST HAVE BEEN CLARA'S, was parked in front of the open shed where Gabriel's Zodiac was kept, its nose in the air. Ania let Jean-Louis take her bag. The field was yellow with leaves that had fallen during the afternoon rains; the damp grass wet the canvas of her shoes. It was still daylight, even though the lights along the roadway were visible behind the foliage. Jacqueline must have been keeping watch for their arrival for she approached, in boots and an apron, using a newspaper to protect herself from the drops of water falling from the trees.

She always wore her hair very short, tightly curled, and a scarf hid her thick neck, whose skin was sensitive to the sun and to emotion. Ania intuited that she was as disturbed as her husband and just as slow as he to forgive her for having been absent so long. For a second her eyes, bright with tears, questioned the expression on Ania's face. "It's unthinkable what happened, unthinkable," she said with bitterness, suddenly taking her hands. Ania could feel her thin lips brush her cheek in a kiss that was as swift and sparing as it had always been. Jacqueline had taken care of her when she was small with irreproachable loyalty. She had never been tender but had shown great concern, a mother's concern. But the couple's love was primarily directed toward Gabriel. Their admiration for him was exclusive and, in a way, contradictory, at least during the first years of his widowhood, which had been cynical and disruptive. Her own suffering and her shame hadn't been understood, her setbacks in school criticized as being a form of incomprehensible stubbornness. "You worry your father," Jacqueline had scolded her while signing her reports.

Their loyalty had been rewarded. Gabriel had finally reconciled himself to their values, agreeing with them little by little, condemning the construction of factory outlets at the entrance to the town, the disappearance of the last local businesses, and later, the poor quality of television programming, the filth on the crowded trains arriving in Saint-Lazare, the invasion of hooligans from outside the area who arrived at night in loud cars that were certainly stolen, young men somewhat like Novak had once been. In one sense, Gabriel's suicide confirmed the threatening debacle ushered in by a world in which they no longer felt safe or in their own element.

VIOLET REFLECTIONS STREAKED ACROSS the windows of the double doors to the living room as Ania entered. Clara was sitting at Gabriel's desk, her features hollowed, her hair a bit greasy, the concerned affection of the previous day visibly distracted by other concerns. "He's in the bedroom," she said with a misplaced naturalness upon seeing Ania at the door. "I have to make a phone call," she explained, her cell phone in her hand. "Can I leave you to yourself?"

Ania hadn't expected to see Clara so at home in

the house or to experience such discomfort. Two of the large sofas had been reupholstered with a light-colored woolen fabric, the old double curtains of heavy jute replaced with an ecru linen. Ania cast a final eye around her, then went to get her bag in the entrance hall, where Jean-Louis had placed it. There, everything had remained as it had been, as if for all eternity: the frog-mouth umbrella stand, the mildewed raincoats piled in the curve of the railing, the bags of stale bread for the horses under the stairs, the keys to the shed, to the Audi, and to the bicycle locks hanging next to the electric meter. The door to the toilet had been sealed and the wall entirely redone. Her father had changed his life after her departure, she realized, believing that, in a way, she no longer owed him anything.

It was Novak who had encouraged her in her desire to come, volunteering to stay with Théo until the following day. He felt that she shouldn't let Clara decide everything, that she had to find the proof that the drawing was hers. Almost immediately,

Ania had regretted talking to him. She needed to allow her worries to take their own course.

THE DOORS ALONG THE UPSTAIRS HALLWAY were open to the inhospitable shadows of the rooms. Ania realized at once that the body wasn't upstairs. All the same, she pushed the door of her parents' former bedroom, which then became her father's alone. A paperback lay in the folds of the comforter neatly arranged on top of the bare mattress. Two crumpled summer hornets were lying on the edge of the window whose closed shutters were covered with white smudges. A cracked bar of soap sat in the shower in the bathroom, from which everything had been removed except for a pile of clean towels, a shell filled with small bars of hotel soap, a mosquito trap and a strip of blue refills wrapped in silver foil.

Ania took her bag to her old bedroom at the end of the hallway. Her name was still on the door, but all her belongings had disappeared, with the exception of a Kandinsky reproduction brought back by her godfather years ago. Even the bedspread had been replaced. Ania stood there, speechless, her face burning. It must have been Jean-Louis who had been given the job of removing her things. To take them where? To the dump? Ania was unable to even comprehend what that could have meant to her father to do something like that. It assumed a form of suffering or defiance on his part that she was unable to imagine. The inventory of what had disappeared slowly forced itself on her. Photographs of her as a girl and her mother at twenty, school notebooks probably, brush and ink drawings that she must have spent hours on after school, pictures taken with Chloé, and probably letters and documents whose disappearance left her feeling vulnerable. Ania placed her bag on the bed and opened the window. Jacqueline would be able to tell her what had happened; she was honest enough to tell her such things, even when unpleasant.

A station wagon was passing through the open gates, cautiously driving over the grass until it was behind the Audi. Ania didn't recognize the young man who got out and went directly to the caretakers. She could hear Clara's voice through the open door of the narrow interior balcony, which overlooked the living room at the end of the upstairs hall. When she was small, Ania had spent hours here, hypnotized by the depressing spectacle of her father's silent and solitary work. She bent over the balustrade. Below, Clara had her back turned to her and was making a phone call while delicately dabbing her eyes before the chimney mirror.

Ania waited a few minutes before going downstairs. Clara took advantage of the time to say goodbye to her interlocutor. She wiped her lip with the back of her hand, saying, yes, she'd take care of herself. "I have to leave you now," she added in a low voice, before hanging up. Ania watched her dig into the box of Kleenex on the low table and blow her nose furiously. "It's so disgusting," she said aloud, as her face broke into sobs. What was disgusting? Ania didn't ask; she never felt sure enough and didn't have the taste for fighting. Neither was she that curious about Clara's convictions. Her pain, however, impressed her, it seemed so unlikely.

The man Ania had seen enter the caretakers' home reappeared in the garden. He climbed the steps until he reached the double glass door of the living room, against which he placed his face. In the backlight, his silhouette was completely black. Clara crossed the room with long strides. "I have flowers to deliver," he announced aggressively, reacting to the alacrity with which she had stepped before him. Clara excused herself: he had given her a scare. "Foolishly, I got scared," she repeated, before opening the doors wide for him, first in the living room, then in the former library, which Ania discovered had been transformed into a bedroom.

The body was lying there, in a corduroy jacket and light-colored pants, on a large double bed recently made with a plaid bedspread. From a distance, Ania noticed that he wasn't wearing a tie and had on shoes but no socks. The tears that rose in her eyes caught her by surprise, the result of some unknown chemistry. Clara had followed the deliveryman into the bedroom. Crossing before the bed while pointing out where the flowers should go, she placed her hand on Gabriel's ankle, which she squeezed, hard, as if she were trying to comfort him with her presence. Ania couldn't get over the fact that such a simple and forceful form of intimacy was possible with her father; it was as disturbing for her as seeing him lying in bed. The man returned with a third bouquet, which he placed to the left of the others before following Clara to the doorway, where she slipped a bill into his hand with gentle insistence.

Ania had moved to the threshold of the room, which rose up now from some dark and unrecognized corner of her memories of home. Someone had installed a window in the wall where there had always been a closet and bookshelves; it looked out over the peonies, which they must have had planted for the sake of privacy. A velvet-covered daybed faced the door. On it, a comforter lay folded in a heap; Clara had spent the night there, a few steps from the body.

HIS GLASSES HAD BEEN REMOVED, and the wrinkles from his lowered eyelids appeared to be made of plastic. It was the first time that Ania had seen a dead body. This presence so abstract, so denatured, and yet so alive left her more curious than disturbed. She extended her hand, winced at the completely foreign sensation of cold, damp skin. The body was chilled, the face artificially smooth, the mouth wired shut, the cheeks transparent. Ania stood there looking, waiting for him to get up, repeating to herself that he was dead, in the hope of getting some reaction out of her. The pale ankles, of female delicacy, hung loose in his shoes. Clara had gone along with this, his eccentricity of never wearing socks. Ania would not have known how to do such things and wondered what meaning they had. It must have been Clara, too, who had the idea of transforming the library into a bedroom. There was even a small bath, constructed from the old toilets on the ground floor whose orientation had been reversed. That's where Gabriel's shaving brush was found, his razor, a hairbrush with a tangle of white hair, his medications, mixed with Clara's creams and lotions in intimate disarray. In the end, he had submitted to the conformity of marriage. Then he wasn't so much above the trivial matters of daily life as all that, this man who had left her completely alone, or alone with Jacqueline, to face the very concrete problems of tampons and training bras.

Her home number appeared for the second time on her phone. Ania sat on the edge of the bathtub. Théo wanted to know if he could take out the biggest puzzle. The measured cadence of his voice reassured her, as well as Novak's seriousness when he picked up the phone to listen to her answer. Ania was never completely calm when she left Théo with his father. Novak had neither the patience nor the intuition needed to address the uncertainties of a small deaf boy. He was careless about speaking to him face-to-face, had never been able to completely acknowledge what had happened to his son.

They had met at a park in town one July 14 evening. The night was hot, the crowd already a little drunk and restless. Several people had jumped fully clothed into the basin of a fountain. Novak watched them, laughing, with some friends who, like him, had arrived from Serbia, and a cousin who lived outside the city, with whom he had been staying for several months. His smile was distorted by a nagging scar, as if it had been made with a pair of scissors. Ania couldn't take her eyes off his mouth. "What are you looking at?" he said to her from where he sat, getting up to go sit next to her. She was wearing her hair very short then. "You have a small head, a button mushroom," he joked, wrapping a hand around her neck. She had had a couple of drinks, he had had several. His raspy tongue, with the bitter freshness of beer, had slipped in deep against her own. With a kind of obedient obscenity, everything inside her had said yes. She was twenty-five. Her lack of self-assurance had, until then, kept her far from love and men. That night, with him, and for a long time afterward, she had felt no more than a burning, anguished excitation, which was never satisfied.

Novak would disappear for months on end but always came back. This had gone on for two years, during which time, and in spite of everything, a lasting bond had formed between them. The fact of her pregnancy had made him proud, proud and crazy, to the point that Ania had wanted to believe he would stick around. Théo was three months old when the marriage took place. Ania was relieved that Gabriel wasn't there. Until the final moment, she hadn't even been sure that Novak would show up for the ceremony or that it was what she really wanted. The five years they lived together, in a kind of total unpredictability, had made her feel feverish and alive, just as they had been devastating for Théo.

THE BEDROOM SHUTTERS WERE NOW CLOSED from the outside. It was almost night when Ania ended her call with Novak, having made him promise not to go out again once Théo was asleep. An old mirror, one side of which was entirely tarnished, occupied the width of nearly the entire wall above the sink. Ania could see the body, now illuminated by a bedside lamp covered with light-colored fabric. Clara was putting socks on him; she suspended her gesture, surprised at seeing Ania at the entrance to the room. "I don't think people would understand," she said simply, with a voice drained by sorrow.

On the glass panes of the tall living room windows the evening was now nothing more than a red streak, a wound made on the reflections inside the room. Clara had put on a hooded raincoat whose horn belt buckle beat against the furniture. "I have to get my brother at the station and bring the music to the church; can I leave you alone with him?" Ania was troubled at no longer finding her as serene and stoic as she had been at Monceau. "The church?" She allowed herself to show surprise without knowing whether the idea really bothered her all that much. Clara looked at her, and her gaze was filled with fatigue. She sat on an armrest and undid the top buttons of her raincoat, as if preparing for a lengthy discussion.

"It wasn't easy to convince the priest," she said, massaging her forehead, "but we can certainly go back to the mayor to ask him to lend us a small room," she said with a laugh that turned into a sob. She brought her bare hands to her face. Clara remained hidden that way for a few seconds, then drew a deep breath and apologized for having made the arrangements without consulting her. "You were so rarely here," she added, justifying her actions without a hint of betrayal. "Gabriel was no longer the same, you know. He had returned to his more traditional feelings, whatever you might think." Ania was not surprised. Her father had always loved being a bit out of step with his own character. "Do what you think is best," she replied, feeling that she had no prerogatives about the burial. "Are you sure?" Clara asked, raising her eyebrows. Ania watched her as she readjusted her raincoat. The incident, though minor, had revealed a potential enemy beneath the beautiful and cautious face.

ANIA WATCHED THE MINI'S RED LIGHTS disappear through the gate. It was almost eight and the sky was melting bit by bit into the blackness of the trees. Gusts of wind shook the leaves of the birch trees against the wire grating on the front door. Ania rediscovered the silence and the unexpected but intimidating freedom that had been hers on those evenings when Gabriel left to sleep in Monceau. She went into the kitchen and, in the refrigerator, found a plate of chopped meat from Saturday that Jacqueline had prepared for her father. Only one of the three wall fixtures was working, and it did more to darken than to brighten the room. The house was uninhabitable at dusk. Even during those times when her memories were happiest, Ania had spent them in the poisoned air of her father's sudden depressions.

Clara hadn't said how long she'd be gone. Ania threw the chopped meat into the garbage pail and prepared a piece of bread with butter, which she ate in the living room, staring at her reflection in the window. The presence of death nearby had already become ordinary. What earlier life prepares us to confront such an extraordinary experience?

The lamp on the nightstand cast its light onto the cold skin. From the doorway, Ania looked into the room where Clara and he had stayed, leaving the upstairs to friends and hornets. The garden had vanished behind the inverted image of the living room, and she suddenly felt that she was being watched from outside. So she turned off the light. A relief of shadows and silence reappeared before the river on which a few red reflections still floated by. Through the reeds planted alongside the small building next door, two windows pierced the night with yellow light. No one was there. Ania rested her forehead against the glass. The whisper of fear slowly grew calm. In the bedroom, the body could barely be made out. Ania hesitated to relight the lamp but finally decided not to return to the room.

Clara had forgotten her phone, which vibrated for a few seconds in the disorder of the desk, left in disarray by Gabriel. Ania drew closer. The vibration had stopped but the screen was illuminated. It was resting on a letter of condolence, a handwritten letter on government stationery. The handful of other letters for Gabriel hadn't been opened. Ania walked around the desk and sat on the chair from which hung one of his vests. With her foot, she hunted for the switch to the halogen lamp. The room seemed to open up before her, lugubrious and profoundly silent. Ania waited a moment, not knowing what she was hoping to find.

The two drawers beneath the top of the desk were stuffed with a dense mass of business cards, receipts, paper clips, rubber bands, and a stack of photos of Gabriel at this same desk or walking into the wind beneath the trees in the garden. The wall of CDs was about the same as she remembered it. The small box of her mother's jewelry was still there and, next to it, the shelves of orange notebooks. A photo hid the radio speaker, a marriage photo taken in the mayor's reception room. In it, Gabriel, wearing a light-colored suit, was sitting on a velvet bench, his gaze focused somewhere beyond the lens. Clara stood behind him, one hand caressing his neck, the other resting familiarly on the mayor's shoulder, her father, probably, or at least a close relative. She was wearing a fitted dress, sleeveless and seamless, with small gold earrings, and, as always, no makeup. Her relaxation in this setting and surrounded by such elegance reflected a very deliberate, almost willful shattering insolence. Ania was surprised at how deeply she felt wounded by the confidence given off by the picture. She put the photo back and opened her mother's box. Nothing had been touched among the small collection of objects, figurines, and rings, to which had been added the enameled medallion she was wearing the day of the accident. Ania hesitated taking the medallion, but with a somewhat theatrical and insincere desire, which she soon abandoned.

THE CARETAKERS HAD MADE A FIRE, and clouds of smoke now reached the first-floor windows. Ania remained pensive in the center of the empty room, fascinated that she could feel so absent from her own past. She hadn't turned on the lights when she came in, just opened the shutters. Some light reached her from the streetlights and the rapid sweep of headlights over the stone pillars of the entrance gate. Soon, a scooter pointed a white beam of light at the façade, then against the wall of the shed, where it stopped. The driver spoke briefly into a telephone before stepping to the ground and lifting the seat to remove something that must have been a camera, and walked toward the house.

He glanced through the glass panes of the entrance door, then stepped back as if looking for another way in. Ania was about to open her window when she saw Jean-Louis come out without closing the door and walk straight toward the man, his arms hanging by his sides. There was a brief exchange between them, after which the man backed toward the bike, his steps marked by a singular impertinence. Jean-Louis followed him a short distance, repelling him by his presence alone, and stood motionless on the road long after he had left. Ania watched him retrace his steps, tearing up fistfuls of tall weeds to free the wings of the gate, replace the bar, and return to the house, making a sign for her to open the window.

That he had known she was up there all that time made her feel uncomfortable. "Make sure the shutters on the garden side are shut and don't answer the telephone," he told her in a broken voice. "They're shit, real shit." He left to go back home. Ania closed the window. The unspeakable brutality of the scene continued to resonate within her. Only once before had she seen him in this stone-cold fury. It was a spring night, maybe a year after her mother's death. Some drifters had gotten into the shed. Jean-Louis had seen their flashlights through the cracks in the boards; later he said that he was afraid they would set fire to the place with their cigarettes. Gabriel had found him kicking the bodies captive in their sleeping bags. Ania had been woken up by his voice, screaming at him to stop. She had gone downstairs in her pajamas, had been surprised by the coldness of the dew beneath her bare feet and stopped; a still unknown distress had left her paralyzed and in tears. Later, her father had come up to reassure her, still shaking with anger. "He might have killed them," he remonstrated, kissing her hair. The coldness between the two men lasted several months. The lack of understanding was absolute; Jean-Louis had been mortified that his loyalty could be vilified in this way.

Ania wondered how Clara would open the gate from the outside when returning from the station. But she had neither the courage nor the desire to go out at night to remove the bar, any more than to close the shutters overlooking the garden. The electric heater futilely exuded an odor of burnt dust. It would have taken an entire day to heat the floor and ensure the rooms were at least a little comfortable. Her bed was made, but Ania feared the sensation of cold sheets, a feeling of lying down in ice, a memory her body had retained of the ski camps that Gabriel used to send her to every Christmas.

It wasn't yet nine; she decided to call home. Théo answered. Ania heard him shout, "I'll let you talk to Papa," before returning to the TV screen. "They've been talking about your father on the news," Novak told her, yawning. "What a strange guy," he added, without being able to repeat what had been reported.

ANIA MANAGED TO FALL ASLEEP beneath one of her old parkas, which she had found in a closet and in which she discovered a dirty handkerchief and a ten-franc coin. The soft knock on her door drew her from her torpor. Clara had come up to ask if she wanted to eat something with them, that is, with her and her brother, whom Ania heard taking dishes from the cabinets. She told her she had already eaten, that she was tired. Their presence in the house and the incident with Jean-Louis had exhausted something deep inside her, and she was not far from tears. She lay in bed fully clothed without drawing the curtains. Wisps of smoke spiraled through the night before the window. Below, a kettle whistled in the kitchen. Then Ania heard the

PASCALE KRAMER

creaking of the tall shutters that opened onto the porch, near the garden, which her father had never bothered to close, even when he left for town for several days. Eventually, she fell asleep to the distant sound of the television.

The house was silent when Ania went downstairs the following morning; it was still early. The French window was open and beyond stood the thickets, which pierced the morning fog one by one. Clara's brother, in a T-shirt and striped underwear, was looking at a laptop placed on his knees. He had his sister's broad jawline and that same pale complexion, which, on him, gave the impression of a lack of character. "Armand," he said, half rising to offer her his hand above the low table. His eyes glanced in the direction of the bedroom where Gabriel was laid out, with an expression of conventional and minimal deference to which Ania did not respond. The scent of lilies had filled the room as they opened their venomous throats at the foot of the bed among the roses, daisies, and carnations.

The small bedside lamp had been lit again and the duvet pulled down on the day bed. Ania wondered where Armand had spent the night.

He got up to get her a cup of coffee, but seeing her approach the kitchen, he simply told her that his sister had gone out to get the mail. Ania saw her then in the garden, talking with Jean-Louis, probably about the intrusion of the man on the motor scooter the previous evening. Clara was listening, bent slightly forward, her chin buried in the scarf wrapped around her neck. She held a packet of letters, which she tapped against her thigh, and Ania noticed that the diamond had reappeared on one of the fingers that held her cigarette.

She was slightly taller than Jean-Louis and so was taller than Gabriel. Her chocolate-colored wrap clung to her pubis like a skin—a long, fleshy plum that rose high in the well-defined hollow of her abdominal bones. It was the kind of detail that Gabriel noticed immediately in a woman, along with her hands, which he claimed told him everything about her. Ania had known these things ever since her father had begun receiving guests at Les Épinettes—she must have been around ten years old at the time. She was aware of his sophisticated advances, his patient eyes, barely damp with an impassive smile; could imagine him hungrily scrutinizing Clara's splendid body. There must be other photographs, and much more daring than the one on the desk in Monceau. Ania wondered if they had already been removed from the drawers, or if she would find them by accident in emptying the house.

THE GATE HAD REMAINED CLOSED. The wood on the wings, now rotted from contact with the stone wall over the years, sweated black beneath the peeling paint. The tall weeds torn up by Jean-Louis withered in a pile nearby. Together, they gave the appearance of mild devastation. Someone tried to open the gate, then the sound of the bell glued to the wall could be heard—the fact that it even worked surprised Ania. Clara crossed the lawn, wet with water, announcing that she was coming. Her car was parked farther down than the day before, beneath the trees. Ania hadn't considered that she might be expecting anyone. Her unease those weekends when Gabriel had company filled her heart like dark water. So nothing is ever really unimportant, she thought, the best we can do is keep our distance.

In the living room, Armand was trying to light a fire, sparking an acrid flame from the green wood. Ania rinsed her cup and went upstairs to get ready when Clara led a couple into the room. They had the uncertain look of people who are suddenly blinded by a strong light. He was wearing a coat with the sheen of fake astrakhan and she had on a blazer and matching headband that pulled back her yellow hair. "We hesitated for a long time before coming," the man said, excusing himself and revealing the two new faces whom he failed to identify. Ania recognized them, though, especially the man, who was a watchmaker in V. and who, a few years earlier, had had a rather unpleasant disagreement with Gabriel concerning the repair of a watch. Their presence in the room seemed to surprise them as much as it did Ania.

Clara accompanied them to the bedroom, then returned, making a sign to her brother to get off the couch while they paid their respects. "They're Loïc's parents, one of the two boys for whom Gabriel got himself canned," she explained quietly in an unaccustomed tone of voice. Armand drew closer and made her repeat it, listening as he nodded his head, his pinched white lips forming an indecipherable expression.

Ania also remembered the boy, an only child whom she used to see hanging around in front of the shop, then later on a motorbike, riding around the village. He was one of those skinny adolescents in cheap jeans and leather jackets whose faces we never remember. Gabriel called them assholes when their bikes stunk up the path that ran along the property. Later, he felt a kind of pity for them, mostly because of the aimless boredom of adolescence in these half-dead hamlets, where even fresh bread was hard to find. Did he even care which of the boys he had chosen to defend? Ania wondered how the parents felt about the questionable publicity that he had added to their nightmare, when they must have already been the subject of considerable curiosity. Had they come to pay a debt to him for a support that had never been requested or anticipated, or to expiate their indirect responsibility in the man's death? There was considerable irony in thinking that Gabriel now found himself making common cause with these petty local people, whose vulgarity and narrow-mindedness he had so often ridiculed, in this same room, back when he was untouchable.

The couple was coming out now, excusing themselves and thanking everyone once again. Ania couldn't take her eyes off the woman, who crossed the living room without placing her heels on the parquet or looking at anyone. Emotion ran down her neck in large waves. Her son had been arrested a few weeks earlier, but her suffering already appeared to be fixed in bitterness and resignation.

Clara accompanied them to the entranceway and

stayed a few minutes to talk. Ania saw her in the shadows, tall, attentive, and present, exactly as she had been with her in Monceau and with Jean-Louis recently in the garden. She understands people, she realized, something very human, and she wondered if her father had admired or ridiculed her for it.

ARMAND HAD CLEARED THE DISHES from breakfast and had just gone back upstairs when Clara entered the room. Her attitude had congealed, hardened. She had her back to the chimney and was facing Ania, her arms crossed, as if she had waited a long time for this. "I don't approve of the murder of that man, that Comorian," she blurted out, her eyes a bright flame. "Your father didn't either, you know. I don't believe everyone should be welcome here. My family is well-off, I've had a good education, for which I'm grateful and which I also wish for my children. Don't ask me to agree to give it all up for people for whom none of that would matter." Ania had nothing to say in reply, nor was she able to find her contemptible. She simply realized that she herself had no inheritance to defend. "I'm not asking you for anything," Ania said, her face unreadable. "I know you're not asking for anything," Clara replied, with a hint of irritation. She then tilted her head back, as if she were offering her throat to an executioner. Ania refused to share in that type of blackmail; she wanted to go upstairs, get her things, and leave. But Clara looked at her again, her features suddenly distorted with tears. "The reactions have been so violent, so unanimous, the banishment so casual." She sniffled, as if she were reproaching her. "They even came here, in this room, to insult us. Of course, no one, not one of them, worried about the man who had been drowned. The body was never reclaimed. And no one bothered to ask about the boy, barely twenty-two years old, who was going to be locked up for half of his life." "All because you went to visit them?" Ania couldn't imagine her father making such a concrete and, in a way, charitable gesture. Clara seemed to delight in her surprise. "Gabriel went to see them, of course, what kind of man do you think he is?" Her tone of voice was firm and calm, her features had already begun to compose themselves. She's not the type of woman to commit suicide, Ania thought, or a woman who's going to take the kind of risks that Gabriel always took, without ever considering the harm he caused or the pain he inflicted.

The sun was rising, projecting the poplars' shadows onto the river, the color of light clay. Clara had grown silent. Her words had left a venomous presence in the room. Ania felt tired and worried. "I'm going home; I'll be back Saturday for the burial." Clara's phone began to ring as Ania was leaving the room. "I saw that they'd called, but they didn't leave a message," Clara blurted out, her voice trembling as she approached the living room door, which she closed sharply behind Ania.

Armand was getting dressed in Gabriel's old bedroom. Ania caught sight of his reflection in the mirror of the armoire, in his shorts. His chest was hairless and his delicate nipples shivered. "Excuse me," he said, amused and unconcerned as he leaned over the unmade bed to close the door that had been left open. His scent and the thick steam from his shower had filled the entire floor. Ania assumed that he had his own way of doing things in that room. She closed herself in her own, which now felt very vulnerable because of their mutual assurances.

CLARA OFFERED TO DRIVE HER TO THE STATION; she had already begun to put on her chocolate tracksuit and was tucking her feet into fur-lined boots. The drive was silent. Clara drove fast, one hand on her cheek. The raw light of morning emphasized the grain of her skin. Tiny lines of bitterness drew out the corners of her pale, fleshy lips. Leaving Les Épinettes, she had taken the road near the old sawmill, where the storage sheds were now filled with weeds. Ania thought for a moment that she was making a detour near the cemetery, but she was probably just trying to avoid passing other cars. She was getting tangled in the resentment she had allowed to come between them. Ania was surprised that she didn't dislike her more. But she reproached herself for having allowed her to make all the decisions from the start.

"Did you end up putting us on the announcement?" she asked as she was getting out of the car. Clara said yes without the slightest hesitation, although Ania had never said anything to her about it. She rummaged around in a box in the back of the car and pulled out an envelope that she handed to her. "It's the same text that appeared in the papers, I can give you some if you want to send them out," she added, without insolence. Ania read her name, *Delâcre-Janic*, incredulous once more at still being Gabriel's daughter in spite of everything. Ania hadn't thought about what that might imply for them, especially for the boy, when Clara had showed her the draft at Monceau. At the time, she hadn't even thought to tell her that the name "Janic" had nothing to do with her own any longer. And she must have overlooked the part—the words now seemed threatening—that said that only friends would be allowed to attend the ceremony.

When Ania got out, she placed the boxes on the passenger seat without comment. "It can wait till after the burial," she said, before closing the door, "but I would like to know what he did with the drawings that belonged to me." Clara's entire face changed, as if satisfied that Ania was finally revealing herself. "We'll talk about everything, Ania. I'm looking forward to it myself."

ANIA WAS HOME BY EARLY AFTERNOON. She was no longer accustomed to the stress, and Clara's temerity had exhausted her. The stores were all closed when she passed the exit to the train station, where the empty boxes from the morning market were piled up. The sidewalk in front of the building had been rinsed with a hose and life had settled into the rhythms of sleep until the following day. She found Novak on the phone in her bedroom and Théo with his nose in a console, sitting on the floor in the middle of a large puzzle whose borders remained unfinished on two sides. The blinds had remained shut; the apartment looked as if it had been steeped in a gray haze all morning long. She was surprised, however, to find that the dishes had been washed and the beds made.

She crouched down next to Théo and surprised him with a kiss on his shampooed hair, allowing herself to be knocked over by the tender savagery of his response. He had turned around and gotten to his knees, facing her, examining her eyes like the watcher that he was of her moments of anxiety and sorrow. Ania took his hand and got up. The upheavals of the past two days were beginning to exhaust her vigilance, and she didn't want to cry in front of the boy.

Novak soon joined them in the kitchen, an empty cup in his hand. He looked like the bad old days, like a man up to his old tricks, his body impatient, his eyelids a bit brazen beneath brows raked by a series of fine scars. The comments about Gabriel on the television had made him edgy. But that their names would appear on the announcement pleased him a great deal. "Nobody understood what he was trying to say," he explained sententiously, pulling on the crotch of his track pants. Ania stared at him with a hint of pity. He had so little idea of what Gabriel might have had in mind. With the years, and as she had begun to acknowledge the world of difference that separated her and Novak, no matter what she might want to believe, the ability to wound had passed from him to her. This discovery—the beginning of a slow return to a humdrum existence—had filled her with sorrow.

Théo continued to hold on to her, clinging to her waist, his cheek against the warmth of her flesh, obsessively examining his father, who was standing near the door, the father who was never on time, who had never learned to approach him without making him jump. Novak smiled as he played with the pockets of his jacket. Ever since Ania had told him to get out of their lives, he always seemed to arrange it so that she had to chase him out again whenever he showed up. "Are you going to inherit the house? The place is worth money," he opined, with an expression of candor and boastfulness. Ania said nothing, no longer having the patience for his unwarranted swaggering. For that matter, she didn't know if the house would be hers anytime soon or how Novak could claim anything from it.

THE TWO OF THEM HAD JUST MOVED when Ania had finally decided to bring him to Les Épinettes. They arrived in a secondhand van in which they almost managed to kill themselves a few months earlier. The Ping-Pong table had been brought out. Mixed with the freshly cut grass, the decapitated scabiosa spread their bright purple petals in the sun. Several cars were parked in staggered rows beneath the pollen of the linden tree. Gabriel was having company. Ania had known at that moment that they should have left, but Novak wouldn't have understood. This father, whom he had seen on TV, was part of what made her special in his eyes. And Ania had believed she was protected, because fulfilled, by the kind of transgression that her choice of a man like Novak represented.

It was a hot Sunday in July, too hot to serve the aperitif outdoors. A thin layer of chaff glittered in the light, stirred up by the warm breeze that gave the silver poplars a mirrored sheen. There was a couple Ania hadn't seen since childhood, and a young woman with narrow, boyish hips who had just come up from the river, a wide Indian scarf wrapped high over her bathing suit. Ania knew only Mireille, a dermatologist who had been her mother's confidante. She had been present for all the important moments of their life and for many Sunday lunches. For years now, she had arrived together with a man, friendly and distinguished looking, who, like Ania, almost never spoke during those meals.

Ania's and Novak's arrival had triggered confusion until they reached the table. They had to wait until Jacqueline added the place settings for the conversations to resume. Novak lost no time in joining, assertive and out of place. With each of his interventions, they listened in silence before continuing where they had left off. Mireille observed him beneath her bangs. "He's terribly sexy," she whispered in Ania's ear, her hand pressing amicably on hers. Her comment sought to rectify what was going on around the table. Ania suddenly found herself completely at a loss.

Gabriel didn't say a word throughout the meal, planted in his chair, his fingers lightly touching the edge of the table. His jacket climbed up his back, giving him the appearance of a turtle. From time to time, his unflinching gaze scrutinized Ania, making her blush. Although she was clearly suffering, Novak remained silent. He had stretched his arm out along the back of her chair and caressed the nape of her neck with his thumb in a gesture of ownership that left her feeling weak and cold.

Eventually, she made her way to the garden without waiting for dessert. Her father soon joined her. His hands in his pockets, his face critical and smug, he had asked her if he should conclude from this surprise visit of hers that she was going to marry Novak. "Maybe I'll even be a grandfather," he joked, stepping back to examine his daughter's waist with the measured eye of a womanizer.

Then his irony darkened. "Is he Albanian or what?" he asked. Ania didn't understand what he was driving at and had told him that Novak was Serb. Her eyes had grown cloudy, her concentration wandered. Her father stared at her in silence, examining her inadequacies with incredulity. "I'm asking you if he's Muslim," he clarified, raising his eyebrows and rising onto the tips of his toes. Ania had no idea, the question seemed ridiculous. Yet Gabriel had questioned her with an air of insolence that was all too serious. That it mattered whether Novak was Muslim or not, or that it might displease him, was something completely novel to her and, in a way, inconceivable.

NOVAK HAD FOLLOWED THE GROUP of guests who had gone out to the garden for coffee. He sat bolt upright in a rattan chair, not fully realizing just how much of an effect he had made. "He looks like he likes it here," Gabriel remarked with deadly pleasure, taking Ania by the shoulder. She hadn't tried to get away from him, not wishing to provide him the opportunity to comment, and together they made their way back to the house as he crushed the layer of dry hay with his toe. "So, my daughter is in love," he said jokingly in her ear. "In love with a worker from the Balkans," he added, with mocking admiration.

They left an hour later, during which time Gabriel had shown Novak the property, engaging in God knows what pointless little game, one from which he himself didn't obtain much enjoyment. Novak returned from the visit strangely agitated and Ania out of love. It was months before she could look at Novak again without feeling the humiliation she had experienced.

When Théo was born, Gabriel had sent Ania a rather generous check together with a long letter, lovely and rambling, in which he explained how much her systematic choices against him had pained him. A few weeks later, he showed up at her apartment. She had only just begun to get used to the baby. Not really believing he would come, she hadn't bothered to get ready. When he saw her dressed as she was and no longer thin, he appeared to hesitate before coming inside. And yet something intimidating had come between them in that moment spent in an inevitable proximity of skin and scent. Gabriel had been curious about the newborn, had taken him in his arms briefly, moved to rediscover the negligible weight of a life that you could hold in your hand.

The building faced the large bay windows of a municipal pool on which floated the reflections of the water. Beyond was row upon row of buildings, which stopped at the yellow fire of a bed of colza dominated by two interchanges. Gabriel had remained at the window for a long time. Ania had watched him rummage in his pockets and check his car from time to time. He was as solemn as he'd been in his worst moments of defeatism. "My generation is guilty of this ill-considered urban planning," he concluded gravely as he turned around. "Our civilization is collapsing from it, but try to say something and they call you a reactionary." Ania had always felt wounded, even weakened, by such remarks. She made a sign to him to stop and, to her surprise, he didn't insist, didn't retort, aware of how the authority of his judgment meant little here, where he was no one.

A YEAR LATER, WHEN THÉO'S DEAFNESS had been confirmed, Gabriel had suggested to Ania that they meet at Saint-Lazare. He had learned it from Jacqueline, and sought information from friends. He gave her the address of a special school run by a woman named Michèle, who had had amazing results. More than anyone else, he had succeeded in convincing her that she needn't feel guilty. Yet he had still managed to forget that Théo was deaf. The incident came back to her now, creating the same sense of pathetic rage that had brought her to tears in the train while returning from their most recent—and disgraceful—visit.

BECAUSE OF ANIA'S HOURS at the day care center, it was still dark when she had to wake Théo. He had so much difficulty waking to the reality of what he was doing, his body lethargic, disorderly, that she felt like she was hurting him. The lights in the pool created a bluish pattern in the depth of the water. Ania remained wrapped in the peace of this hypnotic encounter for as long as it took Théo to emerge, dress, and slowly focus on the contents of his schoolbag. The school had managed to calm him from the chaos that Novak had introduced into their life. Théo, however, remained uncompromising before the disorder or simple negligence of others. Ania hadn't gotten over his inconsolable rage the day their bikes had been stolen from the garage. His face, childish beneath the straight line of his bangs, hardened when she talked of moving. He didn't really have any friends in the area, but the world for him began here. Ania feared the day when the neighborhood would treat his handicap with the inevitable brutality. Ever since the two of them had been living alone, her life had been organized around her concern for him and him alone. She would have been happy if she had been able to reassure herself about what the future might bring. The new possibilities that enabled her to hope for an inheritance from her father made her impatient in a way she hadn't experienced before. She wasn't sure, however, that it would be an improvement to suddenly become someone else.

The school was barely two kilometers away, and they passed through new neighborhoods, an orderly universe of red roofs, hedgerows, and garages as far as the eye could see. Théo followed Ania, his wheel near hers, with a concentration that never wavered. He was always the first student to arrive. Ania entrusted him to the guard and didn't leave until she had seen his silhouette, with the large schoolbag

on his back, appear in the glass-enclosed hallway
leading to the classrooms. He never turned to wave
goodbye, so suddenly absent from the unwavering
ritual of their intimacy. Ania could never accustom
herself to seeing him delivered alone to the silence.
It was this guilt from which Gabriel had been able
to relieve her at Saint-Lazare: to have brought a
child into the world in such isolation.

Ania arrived early at the day care center, where
she found a mattress with a broken seam lying like
a body over the low entrance wall. One of the children was waiting by the door immediately behind
it, accompanied by his father, which happened
often now, a tall, thin man wearing a kufi on his
shaved head the color of black wax. The two older
boys also attended the center, but inconsistently;
Ania could never figure out what determined
whether they would show up. Their gaze was dense,
strong-willed, and a staleness clung to their clothes,
which were hung to dry on the ceiling of a light-
less studio. Plans were being made to find a new
apartment, but things remained up in the air. The

mother entrusted herself to God or the staff at city
hall with the same angry entreaties. Ania had little
patience for her vindictiveness and her indolence;
it took her several weeks to overcome her anger at
seeing her pregnant once again.

The mattress shone with dew. Ania went to get
rubber gloves to heave it over the garbage bin. Little
Issa's father didn't lift a finger to help her, apparently embarrassed to find himself in her presence
outside the center. The milky stain of a cataract
covered his eyes, making his gaze almost blue. Ania
wondered what he saw. She didn't even know if
he spoke French. He responded to instructions by
slow movements of his raised hand. Ania had never
heard his voice or seen any of the children shout
in his presence. The man carried within him an
obscure and very ancient law that was intimidating.
Ania realized that it was this face of burnished night
that she had imagined, the body as erect as a stave
beneath the long, dark tunic, on the man who had
been found drowned in the river in V. The watchmaker's son had never been a thief, never been very

courageous. Where did the hate come from whose only appeasement lay in pummeling those gaunt limbs covered in a simple cotton garment?

Ania had removed her gloves to take the boy's hand. Motionless near the containers, the father watched them walk away. When she closed the door, Ania saw that he had turned the mattress over on top of the garbage to inspect it thoroughly before leaving, princely and miserable. This brief scene left her with a feeling of annoyance and discomfort all morning long. Issa immediately went to play with the toys. His impenetrable face looked at her from the depths of the room. Ania was not always patient or capable of resisting his hostility. Her concern for these lives of such precariousness, who were showing up in greater and greater numbers, overwhelmed her with anxiety and feelings of antipathy that she was often unable to understand.

THE CHILDREN WERE SLEEPING, curled up on the foam mats spread among the shadows. Ania allowed herself to be overcome by the fatigue and tenderness she felt at the sight of them. They exuded an odor of damp clay, their tranquil faces given over to a state of complete abandon whose memory she would have liked to preserve. The dishes had been washed, Lili, the new employee, had gone out to make a phone call. With her cheek resting on her pudgy arms, Lucia dozed behind her bangs, her eyelids weighed down with blue mascara. She wore the same gingham dress as the day before over chunky boots with colored laces. Ania had had difficulty with her the first few months, with her outsize personality. Yet eventually she grew accustomed to the uncomplicated inconsequence of her moods and her outfits, which had initially shocked some of the parents and upset some of the children.

Ania had said nothing to her colleagues about her father, not even Lucia. She felt it would have been a kind of lie to do so without also explaining who he was. She sat down at the table with her tea. Lucia lifted her head and yawned. "I screwed up last night," she said, resting her other cheek

on her arms. "I shouldn't have let you open up
all by yourself." This happened so often that Ania
didn't bother responding. "I found an old mattress
just before the entrance when I arrived," she told
Lucia. She couldn't get the disturbing impression
out of her mind that Issa's father had contemplated
taking it. Lucia listened as she stretched, revealing
her unshaven armpits beneath the pink-and-white
dress. "We don't force them to stay," she noted,
yawning once more. "They should be sent back
home. Especially the mother," she added, after
making certain that Lili was still outside on the
phone. A balloon of chewing gum burst over her
attractive pout. Ania didn't move and stared at the
steam rising from her cup. She would never have
admitted that she didn't like the woman either,
Issa's mother. The hatred took root here with the
jubilant fury of a conflagration. Ania remained
on the edge of her own. Such remarks, which had
now grown commonplace in the neighborhood,
exposed unsounded depths in her. What kind of

indifference toward their own fear and violence would have led them to risk such a confrontation?

A small silhouette in a flared skirt, her hair in a bun, slowly approached from the end of the hallway. Her mouth, of dark plum, perfectly delineated, chewed on a piece of cloth. "Your phone rang," she said impudently, when Ania approached to ask her why she wasn't sleeping.

It was Théo's school. He had thrown up, he had a headache; he was resting in the infirmary, but someone should come get him. The voice was peaceful, inviting. It stirred up an unsuspected desire in Ania for someone to feel sorry for her and take charge. She said she would be there in no more than an hour. Lucia had turned around suddenly when she heard this and stared at her, cracking her chewing gum. Ania slowly put away her phone and turned to face her. "My father is dead," she said, looking straight ahead. Her voice must have sounded false because Lucia didn't believe her. Under the blue mascara, her eyes shone with malice and a kind of affection. "And when will you be back?" she blurted insolently, as Lili entered the room. "Monday, probably," she said suddenly, without being sure she would return.

THÉO WAS WAITING FOR HER at the entrance to the school, accompanied by a woman whom Ania immediately recognized as the principal. With his knapsack wrapped around his stomach, he refused to look at her, apparently upset at having triggered such an unusual situation. Ania bent to examine his face, marked by large rings under his eyes, and kissed him. From his dry lips she caught the scent of acetone on his warm breath. "What have you done to us?" she asked, standing.

The principal suggested taking them home by car, but Théo insisted on going by bike. She waited until he had left for the bike rack to offer her hand to Ania. "I'm Michèle, I believe you remember. Théo was tired when he arrived, it might just be stress." Her hands, covered with wooden rings, caressed the mauve wrap tied around her thin arms. She was close to retirement but retained the beautiful classical or pagan features she must have had at twenty. Ania had always felt immature around this woman, who was, for all that, very attentive and quite compassionate. She had been shocked to learn, during an incident that took place in the cafeteria, that Théo had found in her a relatively partial ally.

"Of course, Théo can go to his grandfather's funeral," she said, pulling from under her arm the letter that Ania had given to him for her. Her deep-set eyelids, highlighted with golden brown eye shadow, examined her with subtle indolence. Théo crossed the courtyard, pushing his bike along a jagged line. "I had no idea you were his daughter," Michèle blurted out, smiling, friendly, and mysterious. It took Ania a few moments to figure out that she was speaking of Gabriel. The remark had been made in a tone of such familiarity that she was unsure whether to assume that they knew one another. But the moment was already over and as if lost, for Michèle bent toward Théo without waiting for Ania's reaction. She placed her hand on his forehead and said, "See you tomorrow," with an encouraging wink, a sign of an extraordinarily heartfelt and adult complicity.

Théo rode ahead, emboldened to be going home at this unlikely hour. Their speed cast shadows beneath their wheels, between which he slalomed with an unsteady rage, his behind raised above the large seat. Whenever someone approached or a group of people slowed down at the entrance to a building, he placed his feet on the ground and turned around while he waited for her. The back of his T-shirt was dappled with sweat when they reached their building. Ania gave him the keys to let him go up and change while she put the bikes away and collected the mail.

There were two letters. One had been sent to Les Épinettes and redirected here, by Clara most likely, for Ania didn't recognize the writing. The other was from Jean-Louis and Jacqueline; it must have been mailed shortly before Ania came by the day before yesterday; they seemed worried that she might not have known or would refuse to stop by. Their distress revealed itself discreetly. Ania reproached herself for not having been more thoughtful with them. She hadn't imagined they would write. This intrusion into her home left her feeling uneasy. She placed everything on the table and unwrapped an aspirin tablet for Théo. He was in his bedroom, putting on his pajamas with somnambulistic lethargy. Ania flicked the light on and off in the hallway, indicating that he should join her.

The excitation gave way to a form of torment that he concealed quite well but that his speech betrayed. Ania took his hands and closed her eyes, inviting him to slow his breathing until he could form sounds without shouting. Théo complained a bit, then made an effort to comply. It was the school that had convinced them (and especially Novak) that it was important for him to speak, that it would open him up to the outside world. Théo advanced rapidly but without ever developing any confidence. He didn't have the temperament necessary to be comfortable anywhere but within the world of signs. Believing it could have been otherwise would have meant lying to him and to herself.

Théo had gone silent, concentrating on the fizzing tablet dissolving in his glass. Ania tried to determine if it had been his teacher who had given the letter to the principal, and if either of them had said something. Théo told her he didn't know anything, making a kind of forced grimace. Sometimes he really annoys me, Ania thought sadly. She went through the days, one by one, without thinking too much about what Théo would do as an adult with his handicap, his fears and obstinacy. Sometimes a chasm would open up and she would be overwhelmed by morbid thoughts for days on end. How could you arrange things so your child wasn't the center of your life? Ania had asked herself that question many times, and more with respect to Jacqueline than to her father.

Théo got up to add more water to the whitish mixture. The silken strand of hair he had been growing on the back of his neck had been cut short, probably by Novak the day before. These paternal interferences didn't sit well with Ania, no matter how insignificant, no matter how trivial. At the time of the divorce, she had imagined, hoped, that Novak would disappear from their lives. But in his own way, he had become an almost regular presence, and she had to accept the fact that Théo belonged to both of them equally.

The boy never said a word about the afternoons he spent with his father, and Ania soon understood that his two lives would remain distinct. Still, she made sure that it was, in fact, Novak who had cut his hair. Théo said yes but wouldn't admit that this had bothered him. His eyes, on which the lie was clearly visible, insistently followed the movement of her lips. Ania held his face with the tips of her fingers so that his attention was directed at her until his severity was mollified. His fever surprised her and at first she hadn't really believed it. "What did you do yesterday? You didn't want to go out?" she asked. Théo responded briefly, suspecting some sort of trick or trap. Ania eventually realized that Novak had let him watch his grandfather on the news. Théo had mentioned it at school, which was unlike him. Ania wondered what he had understood and what else he had said, if it was this sudden excitation that had made him ill. He turned aside so she would stop asking questions. Ania grew angry with herself for having forced him to reveal information that—and he was fully aware of this—would anger her. His face was again crisscrossed with fine veins beneath the yellow skin. He suddenly retched, leaving a damp blob of mucus in his palm and his eyes wet with a distress out of all proportion to the situation. Ania took him to the bathroom, then prepared his bed while he remained bent over the toilet bowl, vainly spitting up long threads of saliva. When he was sick, he took comfort in the fact that clean sheets had been put on the bed and the living room cushions piled on top. Ania knew that it was from her mother that Jacqueline had learned to make up the bed with fresh linens when she had a fever. Long ago, her idea of happiness had been associated with the rough sensation of clean sheets on her burning skin.

Théo had wanted her to bring him some books and leave him to himself. Ania found herself experiencing an unsettling sense of solitude and freedom. She made herself some tea, which she drank as she observed the hustle and bustle in front of the building. They had gotten the apartment from a friend of Novak's. It was the neighborhood where he had stayed when he first came to France; he couldn't imagine himself living anywhere else. At the time of their marriage, Ania had always lived with a roommate in Suresnes, and she had had difficulty getting used to the neighborhood, which was so far from everything, and the brutality of her relations with the neighbors, spending whole days holed up with the baby. Then an official at city hall whom her father knew had suggested the job at the day care center. Her life here had found its rhythm then. Ania had begun to recognize the faces and no longer felt as if she were being seen as an outsider in the building. She even ended up taking pride in her familiarity with these suburbs, which were, in a way, so important at the time.

The other letter was from someone named Kathy, who said she had met Ania a few times at Les Épinettes. She told her how she had been part of the cabal against Gabriel, which she herself qualified as toxic in a confession of sorts in which she explained, in writing that was florid and difficult to decipher, the reassuring feeling of being part of a body, the impression, after the fact, that all of it had been easy but unmarked by any kind of courage. Ania wasn't sure she knew the woman or what kind of forgiveness she was expecting. She recalled an English girl, a tall, thin designer with thick, light-colored curly hair adorned with colored combs, the memory of which had remained tied, in her memory of girlhood, to the discovery of a sanitary napkin stained with blood in the upstairs toilet. What was it they had all admired in Gabriel, and why was he so different from the man they despised today?

THÉO HAD FALLEN ASLEEP and Ania was getting ready to lie down when Novak buzzed and then entered with his key, together with a friend, a man he used to hang around with when they first got married. They worked together on construction jobs, off the books; their hair was still soiled from the dust.

Novak said he'd forgotten a sweater in the hamper. His eyes betrayed signs of intoxication—grass or liquor—that Ania hadn't seen in a long time. To relive the superficial stress of his nighttime comings and goings, which she had submitted to for such a long time, was unpleasant. She told him to hurry up, that Théo was sick. Novak flaunted his annoyance with that disconcerting wounded smile of his that no longer had any effect on Ania, then made a gesture both possessive and familiar, as if to grab her by the chin, before escaping into the bathroom.

His friend was resting against the front door, apparently with the intention of withdrawing from this expedition. Ania watched him, hunched and absent, as he pulled out a package of tobacco from his jacket and attempted to roll a cigarette. Novak was rummaging around in the medicine cabinet, and she shouted for him not to touch anything.

"Tell him they were talking about your father on the news," he blurted with forced casualness as he came back into the room. Ania suddenly felt terribly vulnerable. His friend now looked directly at her as he put away his tobacco. He had pulled out his keys, which he jingled in his palm, alerting them to the fact that he was about to leave. They had come in his car, so he must at least have been curious about what Novak had said about Gabriel to have agreed to go out of his way like this. Ania couldn't understand his unspeakable arrogance, as if it were necessary to undermine the superiority this sudden notoriety gave her, or make her pay for it. Long ago, she had been present when a police station was attacked following the arrest of a local boy. And how could she know that the anger triggered by Gabriel couldn't be traced back to her and Théo?

T HE FOLLOWING DAY, THÉO CONTINUED to complain of a stomachache. He was hot, his head lay like a stone among the cushions. Ania decided to keep him home. Around eleven, Jean-Louis called to tell Ania in his somewhat atonal voice that the funeral was going to be moved up to the following day. "That's what they recommended to us." This "us" included them, them and Clara, in a new kind of bond. Ania could detect, beneath the sententious tone of voice, the disarming pride he felt at being included in their decisions. That was all part of the foreseeable cruelty of things. Clara provided them with greater satisfaction and proofs of friendship than the secretive and deceitful young girl who had frustrated so many of their expectations.

.

When Jacqueline was no longer able to help her with her homework, for an entire year Gabriel had paid a young man to assist her—he was available and very meticulous. Every other day he would come to go over her lessons. He had never shown the least sign of impatience or pleasure in being there, moving his finger like a caterpillar from one line to the next, then waiting, staring at the table in front of him, for her to reread the passage or reply. Sometimes, when he was home, Gabriel came to see if everything was going as it should. Resting with his arms on the table over the open notebooks, he expressed surprise at the useless things they were forced to ingest and made light of the homework they had been given. He had never hoped for much from these classes, had, in fact, never really taken his role as a father very seriously. The slow, heavy little girl she had become, his little country girl, as he now referred to her, could become whatever she wished. Yet his presence in the room left her feeling empty, floating in the fog of what she was supposed to understand. She had never managed to adopt the rhythm of learning. The urgency to respond held her back, her mind resisted, floundered beneath the pressure of a hand that sought to push her forward too quickly.

The school had called shortly before the start of vacation to say that Ania would be left back next year as well. Gabriel wasn't there, so it was Jean-Louis who had come to wait in front of the gates of the playground. "You'll have to tell your father tomorrow night," he noted mournfully, frozen by the profound lack of harmony, the annoying lack of understanding that her refusal to give satisfaction, in spite of the effort and the money that had been spent, had caused them, Jacqueline and him. Nothing more was said during the trip back, and she had assumed that Jean-Louis was far too preoccupied with what she would become. A scorching sun warmed the fetid dust on the seats. Ania was sick to her stomach and, from that moment on, she had had the impression of falling ever deeper into a pit of neglect.

Gabriel had called that evening; he was abroad

but his voice felt close, as if he were speaking directly into her ear. He had been told about her grades, of the faked reports, of the days spent with Chloé. He hadn't been angered by the news; in fact, it had made him strangely giddy. "You're aware that we'll have to find a private school in town. Turning you over to the priests, that should be a barrel of laughs, don't you think?" he joked. Ania didn't understand what he was talking about or why he was joking. She hadn't said a word, only waited stoically for him to hang up. While she was waiting, when there was nothing and no one to comfort her, her heart had felt empty. And it was then that the request formulated itself, unexpected, salutary: she wanted to go to boarding school.

Whenever Gabriel traveled for extended periods of time, Jacqueline would spend the night in his house. After she had served Ania dinner in the kitchen, seated a short distance from the table like the servant that she had never entirely ceased being, she ate her own dinner with Jean-Louis. That evening, Ania had heard her come back around ten o'clock and slip discreetly from the bedroom to the bathroom, ill at ease at being in her nightgown between those walls. The afternoon heat clung to the rooms. Thirst and the feeling of injustice that so unsettled Ania created a stifling mixture. She had spent part of the night at her window. Jacqueline couldn't sleep either and, from time to time, her profile appeared at the neighboring window. They were so close they could hear one another breathe. Ania had let herself cry then, although she knew that it was still too soon to expect any sympathy.

In the morning she had found Jacqueline busy rinsing a bucket of cherries in the sink. Slices of buttered bread were ready on the table. The butter had melted into the cracks and crevices. The sun, which for days now had made the tile floors blisteringly hot from early morning, would make the summer a prison of boredom and solitude. Jacqueline finally turned around, waiting for Ania to sit down at the table. Her reddened hands resting on the edge of the sink and her head arched slightly back, she appeared to be contemplating an inscrutable vision. "Isn't your father lonely enough already? And you want to go away to boarding school?" she exclaimed, her voice broken by sorrow.

Nothing had been explained or forgiven at the time, and later it had been too late. Ania returned only for vacation; most often it was Jean-Louis who came to get her at the station. They could find little to say to each other; Jean-Louis didn't have much to tell and Ania preferred to keep her new life to herself. She had no reproaches to make, however, for it would only have led to misunderstandings and regret. Hearing Jean-Louis on the phone that morning, so overwhelmed by the circumstance that forced them to hasten the burial, conscientious and sincere as well in his desire that she be present, Ania thought they might never see each other again and that the idea must seem as inconceivable to him as it was to her. "I'll come tonight if I can find some-one to look after Théo," she promised. "If only to pick up my things, if there are any left," she added with almost mechanical bitterness, but Jean-Louis had already hung up.

SITTING UP IN HIS BED, Théo hadn't taken his eyes off her throughout that brief conversation. His bushy head, having sweated during the night, bobbed up and down with fatigue and despondency. Ania could deceive him about what was going on but not about what she felt; he deciphered her moods with nearly perfect intuition.

She had just put down the receiver when he lay back down, the sheet pulled up to his chin, his eyelids drooping; it was a kind of blackmail so that she might turn her attention back to him. Ania gave in to the need for tenderness in spite of herself. She caressed his damp forehead, slipped her finger over his slender nose and asked him if it was okay for Nour to watch him that evening, until the following morning. The suggestion brought a spark of joy and excitement to his eyes. The young girl lived in the building and had babysat from time to time when he was very little, stopping by to give him a kiss on his birthday. As slender as an obedient child, she dressed in tight jeans and brightly colored headscarves that wrapped around her graceful features, above which sat a mass of carefully gathered hair. There was considerable tenderness between them in spite of her obvious discomfort with his deafness.

Ania tried to call her, left a message, and returned to Théo with an orange juice that he lingered over at great length, fussing with each seed, which he spit out, one by one, into his fingers. He sat there, his head heavy and his shoulders slouched. "You're going to the funeral," he said, sounding offended. "They said I could go." This was something new, this protest. Ania gathered his face between her hands, attempting to decipher what it was that was bothering him. Théo grabbed her wrists as if to prevent her from harming him. The sun ricocheting off the windowpane made him wrinkle his nose. Ania asked him to pay attention to what she was about to say. "Your grandfather made a great many people angry; we're not too sure what's going to happen tomorrow. Your grandfather wasn't such a nice person, you know,"

she added, with the barely conscious intention of
wounding him. Théo followed her lips with a sullen look, his eyes dark with anger. Ania let him
go, shocked to realize that he was looking at her as
if she were being intentionally cruel or deceitful.
"Even the principal said that she knew him," he
grumbled after a while, trying to hurt her in turn.

NOUR ARRIVED EARLY IN THE EVENING, directly
from the library, where she was going over her
homework. She didn't hide the fact that she had
had difficulty getting her parents to let her stay
overnight. Théo's greeting was a mixture of excitement and uncertainty at the idea that she was
going to sleep there, and perhaps he was also a
little intimidated at seeing her without a scarf.
Ania hadn't been able to gain his forgiveness
before leaving. He had gone back to bed, leaving
her with the unresolved impression of his defiance. Walking to the station, Ania tried to reach
Novak to find out what he had put into his head

about Gabriel, wondering what role he was trying to play in this story. She was equally disturbed at the fact that something of him was in the process of making its appearance in Théo.

ANIA MANAGED TO CATCH THE TRAIN around eight. During the final leg, she was alone in a car whose windows were scratched with a maze of initials and drawings. The Mini was waiting at the back of the empty parking lot, in a corner bordered by a wall of hawthorns. Clara was on the phone. The screen illuminated her face, which was resting on her arm lying across the steering wheel. Ania wasn't sure that it was her Clara had, in fact, been looking for, and she was certainly not prepared to engage in the frank discussion they had promised each other.

Clara hung up and sat erect as soon as Ania opened the gate. She removed her bag from the seat, then unexpectedly extended her hand. The handshake was firm and warm, her smile now accustomed to surprise and sorrow. "I hope it wasn't too complicated to take off during the week. Did Jean-Louis tell you?" she added after a beat, as they were leaving the parking lot. "A petition has been circulating to prevent Gabriel from being buried in the village." The sentence had broken off in the rancor of shocked sorrow. Ania was surprised by this show of innocence after all they had stirred up—it was clearly their own fault—and which now manifested itself in the form of defiance or, at the very least, incomprehension. "You should have seen it coming," she noted calmly, even if she too found the idea of a petition shocking. "Yes, we should have seen it coming," Clara repeated, shaking her head, as if the remark confirmed her divorce from the rest of the world. She rolled her neck against the headrest, wiping her nose with the back of her hand from time to time. "We told hardly anyone," Clara said, turning to Ania as if to reassure herself that she hadn't told anyone either. "Just close friends and some people from the area, most of whom were shocked," she added, as if overwhelmed by their loyalty. Ania had never seen Gabriel frequent anyone from the village, in which he took at most a theoretical interest. But perhaps, in spite of everything, the proximity of his lifestyle, at least back when prominent individuals would come to Les Épinettes, had flattered the inhabitants, and, even more so, his solidarity at the moment of the local community's condemnation.

Clara pinched her lip, which had gone entirely white. She had again taken the road through the old sawmills. Bats skimmed the roofs of the buildings with an electric whisper. The entire day had felt like summer. Ania lowered her window and opened her hand to the wind. The coolness of moss and rain-soaked wood caressed her with a damp veil. Ania had very old memories of coming back from a walk with her father at this same time, when their footsteps could be clearly heard as night fell along the road. "I had forgotten this calm," she said as the car joined the roadway. Clara smiled, as if suddenly relieved by the sense of gratitude. There were no lights, not even another car. She cut the motor and the headlights, placed her hands on the steering wheel, and stared straight ahead.

They waited like that for several minutes, listening to the emanations of the surrounding countryside. Clara must have spent her vacations on the grounds of a property much like Les Épinettes, the kind of place passed down from generation to generation or that can be seen falling into ruin on the outskirts of a village. That much was obvious from her habit of wearing boots, her sense of ease with the real world, as if they were related. This troubled Ania, awakening a feeling of class affiliation that was unfamiliar to her.

In the distance, the wall of ivy of Les Épinettes bordered the horizon with a dark line out of which erupted the ample foliage of the lime trees. "Are you going to sell?" Clara asked, flicking the headlights on again. Ania didn't expect to hear it this way, that the house was going to be hers, and she was overcome with a sense of apprehension and excitement. "Yes, of course. Did you think I would want to come back here to live?" she said with some irony.

Clara smiled. "It's not the worst place to live." As if even her regret for the house, from which she had been torn away, no longer meant anything to her. "And your son?" "In any event, there isn't even a school for him around here," Ania replied, astonished that Clara appeared to understand. She went farther, "Was there ever a chance that you and Gabriel might have children?" Clara remained impassive for a moment. Then she started the motor and turned to Ania. "Your father would have liked to see his grandson from time to time, you know." Ania's indignation caused her to sit up. "And what stopped him from calling?" "Why, you, your attitude," Clara replied with terrible gentleness.

The lighted skylight in the roof illuminated the smoke that climbed above the tiles. The Mini started forward, bouncing down the stretch of rutted road that ended at the gate. Clara honked. Insects hurled themselves into the halo of light in which Jean-Louis's dazed face soon appeared between the wings that he opened wide before them.

Clara parked some distance away to leave room

for the friends who would arrive the following morning. They didn't say another word, both of them too upset, too on edge. The front of the house rose before them like a specter with its eyes closed in the night of the garden. Ania took a few steps in the damp grass to calm down. She thought she saw a fox slip into the little copse of hazelnut trees where she used to hide as a child but that was now smothered in nettles like all of her old hiding places.

Jean-Louis had made a fire. The embers nested softly beneath the rising flames and fine scales of white ash. All the curtains were closed, the bedroom doorway had been hung with a sheet. Somewhere, a radio broadcast a stream of music. Ania put her bag in the entranceway and went to get a glass of water in the kitchen. Upon returning to the room, she noticed that the two small pictures, almost twins, representing a stream illuminated by the supernatural silver of the moon, had disappeared. Clara walked through the service door.

She placed two bags of shopping on the table, put the yogurt in the fridge, and stood next to Ania to observe the void left by the two paintings.

"Gabriel gave them to me," she said, gathering her hair behind her head with the gesture of a swimmer. "Your parents bought them when they first got married, along with the three Degas," she insisted. "They weren't part of your grandfather's collection, which was cataloged and appraised, which is yours. Gabriel knew that as well as you. I have nothing to prove that he gave these to me. I gave them to my brother yesterday so that he would take them with him—I'm very attached to them, and you never know, what with all the hatred around here. If you want, I'll have them brought back tomorrow." Something hard in her had insinuated itself beneath the sense of tragedy. Ania told her she could take whatever she wanted; suddenly it all seemed so pointless and sad. She had noted that Clara had removed the small diamond on her finger, maybe to have her brother look after it along with everything else. Did she think the house was going to be stripped? Ania had a hard time believing that things had gotten to this point; she felt guilty for having been oblivious all her life to what was going on in the world around her.

THE SHEET DRAPED ACROSS THE DOORWAY felt like a presence behind them. Ania didn't know whether it had been placed there to prevent or to protect, unclear how the body could stay there all this time without beginning to smell. Clara had arranged two place settings on the low table, not far from the fire; she appeared with two glasses, an open bottle, and sandwiches on a platter. "Serve yourself," she suggested, softly reclining against the cushions. Ania didn't drink wine but cut half a sandwich, leaving a smudge of butter on her fingers. The telephone began to vibrate and Clara silenced it immediately. Ania didn't bother to interpret her apparently insistent desire to appear friendly. "It's my mother, I'll call her back. They've decided to come. It wasn't easy to convince them," she added, pouring a glass of wine. "Ever since he retired, my father has been the mayor of a village nearby. They were often seen together with Gabriel when he had decided to run for office here. That's when we met. But even for a man like my father, who is far from an idealist, Gabriel was no longer someone he wanted to be seen with." She laughed, a provocative laugh, but maybe also one of revulsion at the thought of what her love and loyalty to Gabriel, in spite of his overweening arrogance, his contempt, his excess, had brought her in the end.

Jean-Louis placed an armful of firewood next to the chimney. Clara wiped her mouth and rose to catch up to him in the hallway. He turned around with a movement that was both servile and content. Ania had never seen him really smile. His was the tight smile of a prude, which cut his cheeks with two vertical folds. Clara led him into the kitchen, then returned shortly after, excusing herself for her absence.

"I forgot to tell you something the other day," she began after again settling into the cushions.

"You don't have to say anything, but I wanted you to know. The watch shop owned by Loïc's parents was attacked several times in one year by a gang who came down from the *banlieu*, black kids, forgive me for putting it like that. It happened again yesterday evening. That guy was hanging around; he ran off when Loïc and his friend challenged him. These people are fed up. They're tired of being spit on because they stand up for what they built here in these villages that no one much cares about. This crime disgusts me as much as you, but accept the fact that I also understand the anger that some people around here can't let go of."

In fact, no, Ania thought, the crime itself didn't disgust her, or not that much, as if there were a shorter step, a lesser evil, than dying friendless and homeless, like that man in his boubou, wandering around in the fields of damp, broken earth. In fact, hadn't Clara said that there was no riot after his death, that no one had claimed the body. The only trace of him would have been his nationality, appearing among the list of names from the shelter that he left in the morning to go who knows where, driven by some kind of determination to get there. Ania assumed that her father must have used this idea of pillage and abandonment for his campaign. Suddenly, she wanted the conversation to be over and for Clara to keep quiet, afraid the woman's convictions might affect her.

Clara got up to stir the logs, generating sparks. She remained bent before the flames, biting her lip. "In any case, it was time for the funeral; with all the heat we've been having, the body's taken a turn for the worse," she said, coming over to sit down on the edge of the sofa. She bit off a mouthful of sandwich, which she chewed slowly without swallowing. "They're supposed to put him in the casket here at nine. We'll leave right after. I'll sleep there," she added, pointing to one of the sofas next to the office. "The bedroom has become uninhabitable." Until then, Ania hadn't thought too much about how things would go the next day. She admired Clara's competence and efficiency, but where did she learn it and from whom?

Novak had called twice. Ania moved away from the windows to listen to his messages. Mechanically, she opened the curtains to observe the night, but the shutters formed a screen before her. The house had never been barricaded before and Ania wasn't accustomed to seeing her father's world so diminished.

Novak wanted to know the time of the ceremony; he was planning to pick Théo up by car early in the morning. Ania couldn't believe that the boy had been so stubborn that he had made Novak call and it was too late to tell them not to come. It all felt so distressing, so tiresome.

Ania could hear music coming from the bedroom. She pushed the sheet aside and felt a shock of compassion on seeing Gabriel there, stiff, his hands on his stomach, his shirt collar buttoned too tightly. A candle burned next to the night table lamp, along with a green spiral that deposited its ashen trace in a saucer. A sweet odor remained in spite of the light scent of citrus. The lips had opened a few centimeters, a black fly was busy on the eyelids. The sheet was supposed to offer protection from the odor and the insects. What chemistry enabled the body to maintain itself for so long? After several days, there was something barbaric but genuine about being exposed in this way. Ania couldn't get over the fact that Clara had stayed here alone, loving and prepared to face the ongoing decomposition. That she had suddenly backed down was not without grandeur. Clearly, it was something she had to confront to free herself from this body she had loved.

Upstairs, her room had been aired out and the bedspread replaced. The heat was on, the old parka she had found two days ago was now on a hanger looped around the window pull. Someone had brought up a bottle of water and placed an ironed bath towel on the back of the chair. These discreet attentions, Clara's doing, certainly, forced Ania to assume her share of the grief. She leaned out the window; shutters clattered somewhere along the façade. Those for the caretakers' kitchen were not closed yet. Jacqueline was still doing the dishes. Ania could see her in profile, bent over the sink, undaunted and dedicated to the task, as she had been after the death of her own child.

It was late but Ania decided to call home. "We're playing cards," Nour told her in that voice of forced gaiety she had with Théo. "I think his fever is gone. Novak was here earlier this evening, the boy made him come." Nour was under the impression that they had always planned to go to the funeral. Ania tried to hide her anger, not wanting the girl to feel bad for having been complicit in something that shouldn't have happened. She was overcome by a sudden sense of panic at the idea that Nour would eventually find out who this father was who was being buried. It seemed inexcusable that she might lose her affection because of this.

OUT AMONG THE BUSHES, A CREATURE, a hedgehog most likely, was walking on the leaves with what sounded like a human step. Jean-Louis had gone

to take the garbage pails out to the road. Returning, he stopped to consider the lawn he had carefully raked that day. Ania waited for him to raise
his eyes toward her window, but his attention was
on the following morning and, maybe, this rus-
tling creature as well, so astonishingly near and
present in the darkness.

Before going to bed, Ania walked along the
veranda at the end of the hallway to ask Clara
to wake her when she got up. The lights were off
downstairs, except for the lamp near the body,
whose white halo pierced the sheet hung across
the doorway. Clara was sitting at Gabriel's desk
wearing a long T-shirt. She had placed one of the
drawers on her knees and seemed to be sorting
through the business cards.

T WAS NOT YET DAWN. Ania had woken early, apprehensive about the day, for which she felt completely unprepared. The hearse was already there, beneath the trees. One at a time, Jean-Louis in his black suit collected the round leaves, like coins, that had fallen from the birch trees during the night. Ania hadn't thought of bringing anything special to wear to the ceremony; she didn't know which, her body or her heart, made her submit to the convention to be present.

Downstairs, the sofas had been pushed aside to leave a passage to the bedroom, and the breeze raised the white sheet like a billowing sail. Clara wasn't dressed yet. She had just had time to slip on a pair of jeans under her long T-shirt. With her hip resting against the dresser, her arm wrapped around her bust, she was talking with a tall man, somewhat stooped, whose face Ania was shocked at recognizing, a handsome face swollen by alcohol. He was an editor, someone from the circle of friends that her mother had made among the neighbors when they had bought Les Épinettes. He had assiduously accepted her invitations and was very fond of her, it was said. As he took Ania's hand, she felt the insistence of a poignant loyalty.

Several worn, orange-colored notebooks had been taken off the shelves above the desk. It had been Gabriel's wish that they be published, and she realized that this had been the focus of the discussion. Clara had taken a step back to let her in on the conversation. With the tension accompanying her welcome, Ania understood that Clara was intent on publishing them but couldn't make the decision without her agreement.

"These are for the last two years, Christian already has the others," Clara noted with a smile. "They're magnificent," she added, alluding strongly to the fact that Ania had barely glanced

at them. Maybe she felt authorized to dispose of
them precisely because of her negligence. Yet Ania
had always known about the notebooks, they had
always been accessible. Gabriel had started to
take precautions after his wife died. Ania learned
of her mother's death indirectly from Jacqueline,
who was mortified that Gabriel had meticulously
described the woman's lengthy suffering, lying
there for more than an hour in the dust at the edge
of the road, slick with blood, her expression one
of shock (from the pain or the idea that she would
die now and in this way), her summer dress sliced
by the sheet metal where her stomach had been,
the dark violet coils tumbling out like a newborn.
He had continued with the same egotistical preci-
sion to chronicle her life, their life, until that terri-
fying moment, as well as his resentment at having
to change the sheets when Ania had had her first
period as she turned eleven.

Of course, Clara had no idea that one could
suffer in this way from someone else's indifference;
she who had never disappointed anyone. To feel

authorized to appropriate such intimate details
was a sign of great presumptuousness. "Do you
ever feel compassion?" Ania calmly blurted out.
Clara burst out laughing, a short, hysterical out-
burst. "I didn't see you shed any tears," she shot
back, suddenly erect. "You let years go by without
a word. You're the one who can't love; you don't
know how to be generous." Her virulence seemed
to erupt from a well that had been filling slowly
for days. Ania couldn't get over her hypocrisy.
"And now you tell me this?" Clara reacted with a
slightly deranged smile. "I've tried to understand
you." Christian stood there listening, motionless,
his head tilted to the side where his large, beautiful hand rested on the wood of the desk. He
attempted a gesture of appeasement to which Clara
responded as if she had touched a burning ember.
The broken veins on his forehead made him seem
vulnerable, a man she must have found cowardly
for his unwillingness to take the situation in hand.
She turned away, then bent over the desk to grab
a large envelope and left to get dressed, offering

Ania a barely audible apology. Christian lowered his eyes. "Gabriel called her several times last Saturday," he said softly to Ania, "but she had taken a room at the airport and had turned off her phone. Obviously, she feels that this wouldn't have happened if he had been able to speak to her."

So Clara had lied that first day in Monceau. Ania was absurdly hurt. She became aware of her assumption of the woman's integrity, as if this were something inevitable, something her pride made necessary. "And that explains why the notebooks have to be published," she remarked, trying to hide just how shaken she was. Christian took her hand in his. "I loved your mother, you know," he confided, as if to attest to the sincerity of what was about to follow. "The first notebooks are very beautiful, even those that concern you. The last must be surreal. Clara thinks they're prophetic. I imagine she's trying to reassure herself by showing who and what really killed him. Suffering makes you a bit crazy," he added, releasing Ania.

THE SHEET ACROSS THE DOOR had been removed, and the warm breath of autumn flowed through the room. The body appeared to have been forgotten next to the casket, placed on a type of folding stand alongside the bed. Armand had appeared in the living room, accompanied by a couple with a newborn, who was sleeping on his father's chest. Behind them, Jean-Louis was cleaning up the ash that had fallen from the chimney, feeling useless and unhappy in his suit. Ania made her way through them to get some air. She hadn't tried to call Novak, hoping he would forget, like all the other promises he had made to Théo. The room was filled mostly with people she barely knew. Nothing forced her to stay other than the stubborn need not to belittle herself in front of Clara. Outside, in the open air, still and golden, with the deep grass beneath her feet, Ania walked down to the small stand of hazelnut trees that she had rediscovered upon her arrival the night before. Snails had left a viscid trail on the low branches, spread out like a skirt. Ania reached up to shake loose a few still green nuts that released an acidic liquid when she bit them. "Don't eat them, they're not ripe," Jacqueline shouted from a distance. She approached, after a moment's hesitation, then stopped a few steps away to look at her, as if disappointed once again, after all these years, at the loss of the beloved little girl. The bitterness and sorrow were embedded on her features. Ania noticed she was wearing new shoes that were already beginning to hurt her feet.

"It's hard for us, you know, he gave us so much," she said, touching Ania's cheek with the back of her hand. "Do you realize that no one knows about the funeral?" She was about to add something, but the sentence remained unsaid beneath the narrow line of her ravaged smile. "All these stories, it's really something." She sighed, and in that sigh, her anger rose and collapsed. Ania spit into her palm the milky bean she had placed in her mouth. "He spent his life looking for stories," she remarked, with all the compassion she was still capable of. Jacqueline shook her head in sorrow, retreating before all that might be cause for regret.

Ania didn't want to insist; it was pointless to continue talking about these things since they didn't see eye to eye. Besides, you couldn't just make it all go away, not the pain and not the attachment that had grown between them over the years, when all of them had done what they could.

"Do you know what he did with my things?" she asked, trying to elicit her compassion for her own wounds this time. "Everything's in the small room in the attic, we weren't sure what you wanted to keep." Jacqueline again moved toward Ania, as if she were trying to rediscover her with the tips of her fingers. "I thought you had thrown them out," Ania said, almost regretfully. Jacqueline looked at her with compassion. "Do you really dislike us that much?" The idea must have troubled her for a very long time to have caused such resentment, and she took her arm for a moment, holding it beneath her own before walking away.

As she went up to her room, Ania passed Clara's parents, encumbered by a tall, noisy bouquet in cellophane. This was the man who had married them.

He greeted Ania with a smile, obviously without realizing who she was. Clara had her mother's features, even the same straight hair, which her mother wore sculpted behind her like a helmet. But it was the only resemblance between her and this couple, harsh and thickset in appearance, for whom she was still the attentive daughter. And confident as well, thought Ania, seeing her finally relent, her shoulders quivering and her face distorted.

ANIA HADN'T HAD ANY COFFEE. A bad headache added to the growing depression caused by her ambivalence about being there. From the garden there arose the sound of footsteps on the fallen leaves. She looked out the window. Jacqueline was closing the shed, Clara was smoking under the cherry trees, taking long drags, her head thrown back. Ania saw her near the angle of the wall, through the red flame of the leaves. She was wearing soft, dark slacks that flowed down her lovely legs, and a beige turtleneck under a short patent-leather jacket with a wide belt. There was something ostentatious and desperate in her attire. Ania wondered what rage within had given her such resourcefulness and coolness in the face of adversity. Voices could be heard on the side of the house, and someone had just rang the bell on the front gate. Clara bent to see whom Jean-Louis was letting in. Novak and Théo had arrived; they were waiting near the shed. Ania wondered how long they had been there and if it was possible that they had come by train and walked from the station.

Théo's bangs were stuck to the side with hair gel. His hand in Novak's, Théo looked around, apparently uneasy at not seeing her or seeing her angry. Ania withdrew mechanically from the window. It was the first time she had had the opportunity to observe him alone with his father, and she no longer recognized him completely. The anthracite fabric of his new jacket shone in the light. Ania couldn't get over the fact that Novak had thought about and taken the time to buy him clothes; she had never known him to be so attentive to his son's wishes.

Clara crushed her cigarette in the grass and came
to greet them. Novak took the hand she extended
toward him. That she seemed to guess who he was
made him blush briefly. The cut of his suit made
him appear a bit thuggish, a bit of an outlaw, which
he tried to conceal by remaining circumspect. Clara,
however, displayed no sign of displeasure at seeing
them there without having first notified her. Standing a couple of steps back, Théo never took his eyes
off her. She was very attentive toward him, placing
her hands on her knees as she bent to greet him.
She was looking at Gabriel's grandson; Ania would
have liked to know what she saw and the extent to
which there was and there remained a generational
connection between them. She guessed that some
part of the innocence with which Théo had grown
to accept their life together had disappeared.

JEAN-LOUIS HAD COME UP TO TELL HER that everyone had arrived and that they were about to put
Gabriel in the coffin. He observed her from the

doorway, incapable of concealing his befuddlement at discovering that she was planning to dress as she had the day before. Ania watched as another car arrived, with local plates, out of which stepped the man who had been her pediatrician for many years. "Look who it is," Jean-Louis said, but without saying anything more. He was folding his handkerchief, which he placed back into his pocket after wiping his eyes, stating that he had to go back downstairs. Bits of cotton fluttered from the dried blood on a cut on his chin. Ania went over to remove them. Jean-Louis allowed her do so, motionless, his neck stiff, a vein pulsing beneath the collar of his shirt.

"Jacqueline told me about your stuff. Everything is upstairs. We can take a look later if you like. We weren't sure you were going to return," he added, still worried she might not believe him. Ania made a sign that she wasn't in a hurry and let him go downstairs. He had changed, he had grown old these past few years, more than she would have expected. His severed fingers gripped the banister with unexpected caution. He was no longer the man who tore out the nettles at dawn, cleared the snow in winter, and came to wait for her every day at school. An infinite nostalgia for everything that had gone wrong in her childhood began to weigh down on her like a stone.

THREE OF THEM STOOD AROUND THE BED to lift the body, which suddenly seemed to stand before them, stiff as a mummy with ashen features, unrecognizable from the rictus of its parted lips. Clara groaned as the body shifted in the arms of a fourth bearer, who placed it with a kind of tenderness in the coffin. When he was carefully settled, one of the men came and bent over Clara's ear, and returned to gather two of the bouquets, which he placed at the dead man's feet.

It was only then that Ania began to grow uneasy about Théo's whereabouts. Standing straight before his father, who held his shoulders as if he were trying to keep him on the ground, he followed the scene with the seriousness of a little pope. He hadn't noticed that his mother was there, hadn't even looked for her and at that moment of that brutal ceremony might even have forgotten her. Ania wanted to understand what had fascinated him so much at the idea of being present as well as the source of the emotion that seemed to unsettle him when the coffin was closed.

Clara held one arm folded over her stomach, her fingers on her chin, in an attitude more of perplexity than pain. She barely reacted to the sound of something—a lamp or vase—that had been knocked over in the living room. The men finished gathering the bouquets while Jean-Louis went to see what had happened. Ania took the opportunity to go out to the garden; the violence she felt was unexpected.

The hearse, parked on the grass, was open. Fleurs-de-lis decorated the satiny padding of the interior. Ania approached and could see her reflection in the body of the hearse, just as Gabriel had seen her for the last time on the train. She realized how much she had let herself go since Théo was born. Soon, all of that would seem far away and harmless, she thought. Half hidden in the shadow of a lime tree, a man was watching her. He took out a cigarette and lit it as he came toward her. It took a few seconds for Ania to recognize Mourad and was surprised that he appeared to recognize her immediately.

He had put on weight and there were thick whorls of flesh beneath his eyes. "Do you remember the photo?" he asked, with that strange, feminine voice of his. "Your father kept it in his office in Monceau; he said you looked like a shaman." Ania replied that she had found it when she had met Clara earlier in the week. She was no longer bitter now but felt that her courage had abandoned her. Mostly, she felt like an orphan.

Mourad smiled affectionately, perhaps trying to determine what remained of the wistful little girl who had so affected him at the time. "What a waste," he said after some moments, turning toward the house. Ania wondered just what had been wasted for this tender and loyal man, who had apparently remained one of the close friends Clara had mentioned. She thanked him for coming, feeling guilty, as well, for his attachment. Théo was leaving the garden, grimacing in the light as if he had just woken up. His bangs, swept to the side, gave him a moonlike face on which his confusion now appeared even greater. He clung to his father, who pulled him over to the side to make way for the coffin.

The gate was wide open again, revealing the familiar landscape of the fields bordered with rust-colored stands of trees beneath the magnificent sky. Clara had made a sign to Mourad to ride with her in her parents' car, and Ania spontaneously followed Novak, who had parked on the gravel outside, anticipating that the seating arrangements in the cars had already been determined. Théo walked on, propelled by his father's hand on his neck. Ania watched as he twisted slightly to look for her. She was unable to explain the resentment she felt for him then.

Novak had had the car washed and had removed the papers that were always on the seat. The announcement, folded in two, was stuck next to the gear shift. So Théo had taken it upon himself to remove it from her bedroom. "He told me you said it was okay for us to come together," Novak informed her, in response to her reproaches. Ania glanced at her son in the rearview mirror. Sitting in the middle of the seat, he was busy flattening the collar of his jacket. It was upsetting to see him become someone, someone she knew nothing about. She decided not to say anything to him. The unending calm of the landscape around them eased her malaise. Novak put his arm through the lowered window, waiting until he understood when to leave and where to go. His jacket tightened around the armholes; he had removed his earrings, and the empty holes formed a painful pattern on his ear. Ania rested her neck on the back of the seat and closed her eyes. Seeing the two of them like this, their sincerity and their eagerness to mirror that other world in which they played no part, left her feeling defenseless.

Clara's parents' car had just passed through the

gate. Clara quickly got out to tell Novak to follow immediately after them. She made a sign of complicity to Théo, who sat forward between the seats, feverish, concentrated, his lips tightened by a thin fold of white saliva. Ania turned to touch him on the knee and pull him toward her. "Are you still sick?" The boy moved his head from side to side but did not look at her, his attention absorbed by the motion of the car. Ania pinched his knee again. "You know, Théo, I'm not going to keep the house, and Clara is going home tomorrow, we won't see her again." Novak had started the car, skidding a little on the gravel; he stared at Ania, surprised by the cruelty of her remark. Théo didn't react, however, focused on what was going on outside, pouty and silent. Ania bent to take hold of his hand. "Everything will be all right in a few hours," she told herself with relief.

At the final intersection before the village, the lead cars turned right to join, just below the railroad tracks, a road bordered with small gardens filled with orange and purple dahlias. Clara had failed to tell them that there would be no Mass. It was another concession made to the petitioners, whose violence and determination Ania was unable to comprehend. Théo's palm was damp and alive in her hand. He had advanced farther between the seats at the approach of the cemetery, whose moss-covered walls rose up among the fields. This stage of the ceremony seemed to demand yet more courage from the boy.

Novak parked away from the other cars. Clara stood with her back to the gate. She was talking with her father, who listened as she fingered a cigarette, trying to convince her of something. Then, suddenly, she moved quickly away, her hands pressed to her eyes in a gesture of such suffering that Théo gripped Ania's shoulder, as if to urge her to do something. The dark circles absorbed his face now and his chin began to quiver slightly.

THE GRAVE WAS IN THE LAST ROW, not far from the other entrance to the cemetery. A backhoe was idling by the side of the hole, waiting to push the pile of yellow clay that had broken apart on the gravel walkway. Ania hadn't expected that things would take such a concrete turn or that Gabriel would be buried next to her mother. She realized then that she had never come to pay her respects. Gabriel had been so careful to keep her away from the drama. The day of the funeral, Jean-Louis had sent one of his great-nieces to play games with her all that afternoon, in an atmosphere of boredom and barely concealed fear. Ania remembered the crowd and the type of euphoria created by the alcohol mixed with the violence of their sorrow once they had gotten over the shock. It had been agreed she would have dinner and spend the night with Jacqueline, but when the time came, Gabriel had lacked the courage. He took her for a long walk along the river, walking silently at her side, his hand pressing her own, and his face breathing in the hot air of summer with that brazenness, that rage for impropriety that would ultimately avenge him for having killed the woman he had loved so much and who had offered him the world.

Clara's friends, those who had come with Armand, waited a few steps away, along with several others from the village. Mireille, however, was not there nor were any of the friends from the Sunday dinners, except for Mourad. Ania noted that a police car was parked near the far entrance, where four young men in ironed shirts now appeared, alongside several girls, whose long hair fell across astonishingly weary shoulders. They must be Loïc's friends, she thought, since they're joining the watchmaker and his wife, who appeared to have been there for a while, standing by the wall. The woman's gaze remained directed at the ground, and she barely made room to let the young newcomers stand next to her. The priest asked several times for everyone in that uneasy crowd to come together. Ania didn't know any of the young men or women.

She imagined that in a few years, Théo would display the same sort of irresolute slovenliness.

Clara turned around to look at her. Seeing that Ania intended to stay in the back with Théo, she slipped her arm beneath that of Jacqueline, which she pressed to the warmth of her own until they were ready to walk to the grave. Gulls had appeared with the first rays of the sun above the hills. They circled for a moment before scattering among the fields like crumpled papers. Jean-Louis allowed himself to be distracted by their arrival. His attitude reflected his deep indignation over the shortened ceremony, which Ania was unable to explain, not understanding who or what, beneath the golden backcountry sky and the falling leaves, was responsible for things being the way they were.

IT WAS LATER, JUST AS THEY WERE GETTING into the car, that a man who had arrived on foot by the road suddenly appeared in the parking area. Ania wouldn't have paid any attention to him if Théo hadn't stood up between the seats to look. The man walked directly to Clara's door, rapped on the glass and, when she cried out, seeing his face there before her, began to insult her. Novak undid his seat belt to intervene, but Ania screamed at him not to get involved. Things were bad enough already; in fact, it was madness to have let the acrimony get as far as it had. The man was rapidly pulled away by an employee of the mayor's office whom Ania hadn't noticed before, then someone ordered everyone to get back in their cars and leave. Sitting next to Mourad on the backseat, Clara remained bent over, her head buried in her jacket. Ania wondered if she had been injured, and her fear shocked her.

STANDING BY THE EXIT TO THE PARKING AREA, his hands on his hips, the man sternly examined the faces behind the windshield. He had a large mop of light red hair mixed with gray, a high, creased forehead, and a dazed look. Ania had no idea who he was. It was almost eleven o'clock and she hadn't even bothered to find out what was happening after the ceremony. A kind of bottomless fear wrapped her in herself, and she wished she had never set foot in her father's world again. Théo, too, had been shocked by the altercation. With his back stiff against the seat and his lips sealed, he looked like he was struggling with a sudden desire to vomit. Ania placed her hand on his flushed cheek, but he pushed it away, intrigued by what was going on in front of the car.

A crowd had formed not far from the other exit to the cemetery, where Ania was surprised to discover that the road had been blocked to cars, most likely just after they had driven through a short while earlier. Among them were the four young men she'd seen with Loïc's parents. Two gendarmes were trying to prevent them from going after the vehicles stopped at the roadblock, while a third instructed the drivers to turn around. The tension was rising on both sides. A few steps behind the group, the young men's girlfriends formed a compact and stubborn wall, echoing the growing anger. Chloé was there, wearing a long overcoat that made her look like a little old lady. Ania hadn't seen her at the cemetery. She was about to lower her window to ask if she wanted a ride, but Théo reacted with such ill humor that she gave up the idea. In any case, she wasn't all that curious to learn who these people were and why they were so angry. Novak parked on the shoulder to allow the other cars to maneuver. He took the time to remove his jacket and grab some mint candy for Théo from the trunk of the car. A small light green van had stopped at the bend in the road below them. There was a woman inside, on the passenger seat, and she had opened her door to observe them.

THEY HAD BEEN THE LAST TO LEAVE the parking area and now found themselves far behind the others. Ania told Novak to take the road alongside the gardens bordering the railroad tracks. Jacqueline had cultivated several of those parcels and used to bring Ania with her when the strawberries were ripe. For a while they had also had a large garden at Les Épinettes, but one day Jean-Louis had turned it into a lawn without anyone ever knowing why. Ania thought that after the sale, she would have neither the opportunity nor the desire to return to the area, a place about which she could recall even the smallest details.

None of the guests had returned by way of Les Épinettes. They found the gate locked, a bouquet of white lilies placed among the rocks against the pillar. Novak insisted on honking his horn while Théo, now crying, decided to throw up against the wall. Ania went with him to hide him from the roadway and hold his forehead. Both of them were shaken by his convulsions. They should have returned home immediately, but Théo was too sick and Ania felt twinges of guilt at leaving the property unattended.

CLARA CALLED SHORTLY AFTER they had managed to get inside and found all the windows open to the garden. She apologized for having lost them. "We waited for you by the old train station, but not for very long given the way things were going," she said in a flat tone of voice. Everyone was at her parents' and they were welcome to join them if they decided to stop by. Her voice was tense, almost flat from exhaustion, not at all welcoming. Ania hesitated before asking if she knew who the man was who had insulted her at the cemetery. Clara responded as though she had been looking forward to the question. "They are idealists," she answered at once with unconcealed contempt. "They've been a pain in the ass for some time now," she added, with a kind of violent sob. "Let them make their mosaics and leave me the hell alone."

Ania recalled that a few years earlier, Gabriel had told her about an artisan and his wife who had moved next door to them at Les Épinettes. He said they were hoping he would invite them over, which must have been the reason for the wall of reeds planted at the bottom of the garden.

Clara blew her nose and then informed Ania

she would probably be sleeping at her parents', in which case she would stop by to pick up her things the following day. She failed to add that she would never set foot in Les Épinettes again, but her uninhibited sniffling said it for her. "The lawyer has your address," she said after she had calmed down. "He won't get in touch with you right away, and there are quite a few debts, especially on the house and the apartment in Monceau." Ania couldn't explain the relaxed tone with which she said all this. "I probably won't be here tomorrow when you arrive," she told Clara before saying goodbye and hanging up.

Novak had followed the conversation from the terrace facing the garden, over which the beautiful light of summer's end spread. Ania made a sign to him that she would tell him some other time. Théo returned from the bathroom looking hopelessly defeated. He was hot, he had a headache, he couldn't throw up anymore. Ania went to kiss his hair. His discomfort joined them to one another once more with a sense of limitless need.

Around them, the misarranged sofas gave the

impression of a recent shipwreck. Ania was a bit upset with Jean-Louis for having left while leaving things were still in disarray. Novak offered to help rearrange the furniture. He was hoping to look around and maybe even sleep there, but Ania felt that their lives had already been sufficiently reintegrated. She accompanied him to his car, parked by the shed, and let him see the Zodiac that Gabriel had put into the water that day long ago and that had impressed him so strongly. The place was absolutely silent when he left. Ania shut the gate behind her but didn't lower the bar. She stayed with Théo all that afternoon, dozing in front of the television, uneasy at the thought of all she would have to sort through, discard, and uncover.

It was around seven o'clock, after Théo had finally fallen asleep in the small bedroom upstairs, that Ania was awakened by the sound of an Audi. Clara wouldn't be coming back, and Jacqueline was in the process of locking the gate. She had slipped on a parka like a cape over her dress and undone the buckles of her shoes. Ania saw her raise her eyes to the bedroom, but apparently without noticing her, then turn back to wait for Jean-Louis, who had gone to arrange some papers using the car's interior light. She appeared calm and distant. Ania watched them enter the house, holding one another by a finger. The house, with all the lights out in the pale night must look to them like a large steamer trunk that had washed up on shore. Ania had an intuition, a very clear one, of the vertigo of silence and emptiness that inhabited them. She felt the approach of a similar apprehension like an immense regret still to come.

ANIA HAD SPENT THE NIGHT with Théo in the large bed in her parents' old bedroom. He had woken up several times, anxious about everything—random vibrations, the stillness, the night's palpable density. It was after nine when Ania got up. She found some sliced brioche in the freezer, several jars of jam, and a chunk of butter that reminded her of the time when her mother was around. The Audi was no longer in front of the house; Jacqueline had left a note indicating that they had been invited to spend the day with friends. In its current state of abandonment, the house sounded different, the atmosphere entirely changed. She went out to the garden to drink her coffee in spite of the wind, which had risen during the night and swept the land with the scent of crumpled straw. It was ten when Chloé phoned. Théo had just come down, pale and angry because he had woken up alone in the bedroom and didn't know where he was.

The grave had been vandalized, splattered with black paint, and the flowers crushed. Chloé said that there was graffiti on the wall at Les Épinettes. "It's your retarded neighbor and the people he brought with him to mess up the funeral. They have no business bothering you, you and Clara. It's liable to cause trouble with the kids in the village." Ania asked herself where Chloé got the information and if Jean-Louis had seen the graffiti when he left or if it had been done when she was alone with Théo. Chloé suggested she tell Clara, but Ania didn't want to have anything to do with it. A gust of wind shook a wicker armchair on the grass, and she thought she heard the door to the shed. She promised Chloé she would be careful and hung up, uneasy about not knowing what to do.

Théo was waiting to find out what was going on, listless and cold before the windows that had been pushed ajar by the wind. Ania told him not to worry and to go lie down on one of the sofas, which she covered with a throw. The boy allowed himself to be pampered. His eyes were rimmed in gray, almost black at the corner of his nose. His tongue, thick and white, contributed to the nausea he complained of. Still, he didn't want to go home, not yet, persuaded that Michèle might yet come, since the burial had originally been announced for that day. He needs so much to be acknowledged, Ania realized, angry with herself for the uneventful life she forced him to lead. Théo began to doze off, his mouth pinched and his cheeks burning. She withdrew her hand from his and sat, pensive, on the edge of the sofa, looking at the tops of the poplars shift with the movement of the clouds. The amorphous sorrow that had accompanied her childhood returned, nearly intact. Maybe she was made of nothing but boredom and anxiety, she thought, as she faced the expanse of silent hours in the stillness of the garden.

IN THE BEDROOM WHERE GABRIEL HAD LAIN, the throw had been taken from the bed and tossed on the day bed together with the sheet that had been hanging over the doorway. Strangely, the presence of Gabriel's corpse these last few days had made his death more abstract. In the closets, built into the wall on either side of the bathroom, Ania found his bathrobe, his odor, his clothes, and those of Clara: short jackets, jeans, narrow, businesslike dresses, many in beige, almost no true color. The evening before on the telephone, she had said she would stop by to pick up her things during the day. Ania remembered the envelope she had seen her take after the discussion with Christian about her father's notebooks. She went to sit at the desk to see what she might take with her. As she expected, the marriage photo had disappeared, together with the sheet of pictures of Gabriel and letters of condolence. Gabriel's mail, however, was still there. Clara hadn't opened it. You could rely on the fact that she wouldn't take anything that wasn't hers. Théo had fallen asleep on the sofa. Ania closed the windows overlooking the garden and went to check on the shed, which was padlocked, then decided to go up to the small room in the attic.

There were roughly ten cartons, scattered here and there, filled with flyers and notices for her father's campaign five years earlier. There he was in his office chair in front of the precious disorder of his wall of CDs, his chin resting on his fist, his acid gaze, his bare ankles delicate beneath the rough cotton slacks. He had always seen himself like that, and it was what he had always been in the end: cultivated, insightful, inappropriately free of pity and convention.

Her things were there, in plastic boxes labeled by Jacqueline, beneath protective covers—her ski outfit, her little girl's coats, and an evening dress of her mother's that had hung for years in Gabriel's closet. A circular skylight filtered light over these dead things that she would ask Jean-Louis to discard—if not him, then who? Ania felt overwhelmed by her discouragement, like a rush of bile in her throat. Outside, the wind revealed broad swaths of blue sky. She rediscovered the wonderful view from the skylight, almost as tall as the poplars. It overlooked the neighboring properties: the high fields littered with straw, large beds of flowers, some late, some gone to seed, a forgotten hammock between two plum trees, and, immediately behind the reed screening, the house of the artisans, whose flat roof had been cleared of the usual piles of rotting leaves and then recemented. Ania recognized the light green van that she had seen the day before on the shoulder of the road when leaving the cemetery. So they were the idealists Clara had spoken of.

THÉO WAS STILL SLEEPING WHEN ANIA came downstairs, his breath sour and hot. She hesitated waking him so they could take the twelve o'clock train and decided to clean up outside while she waited. At the bottom of the lawn, a silhouette was moving among the trees. Ania could make out Michèle's slightly detached hunched and slender frame. She walked lazily, while rummaging in the grass, crossing the garden diagonally and stop-ping from time to time to look toward the house, her arms by her sides, as if she were waiting to be called. Seeing Ania come out to the terrace, she waved her hand. "I'm sorry to come in like a thief, but it was closed on the other side."

She had used the gate along the river, an entrance that had been abandoned to the weeds for years. Small wrinkles brightened the corners of her long eyelids. "It was a year after your mother's death and it didn't last long," she added, seeing that Ania was beginning to understand that she had come here before, but as a lover. "He was so unnerving but so witty. He hurt me, but I can't be angry with him, and I was planning on coming to the funeral," she concluded, backing up, her arms crossed, to exam-ine the façade of the house. Ania couldn't get over the feeling of peace she felt in her presence. "I want to see if Théo is up," she said. "He was waiting for you." Michèle picked up the wicker armchair over-turned by the wind and sat facing the river, her elbows resting lightly on the arms, her hand playing with her bangs, and the gnats circling in the light.

Théo wanted to get up right away, was annoyed that he hadn't brought a change of clothes. His cheeks were starting to take on a bit of color beneath the circles, but his gestures were dulled by fatigue. He had to go the toilet again, then wanted to look for a deck of cards he said he had seen in the cabinet drawer. Michèle rose in a movement of joy, surprised when he came out to join her. She helped him move a small table for his game, taking great interest in what he wanted to show her, then, once he had arranged the cards, she sat down and turned to Ania, who was standing on the terrace steps. "Gabriel called me after years of silence to ask my advice about Théo. Because you weren't using his name, I had never made the connection." Michèle stopped speaking to observe the garden and, maybe, examine her memories. A slight smile spread across her thin lips, colored a dark violet. She looked amused, maybe even touched, by the fact that Gabriel could have had a daughter like Ania.

"What do you think about all this?" she asked, smoothing the wrinkles in her linen slacks, as if she were leaving Ania the time or the freedom not to reply. "We came from the same mountains, he and I, went to the same lycée in Clermont. He worked so hard to erase any sign of his rustic origins and achieve a refinement of understanding that everyone ridicules today. I guess that's what made him so resentful," she added, as if she had to account for her feelings for him in spite of everything that had happened. She had learned from Novak that the funeral had been moved up a day but wasn't able to break her other commitments. "Were you worried it would turn out badly?" she asked, closely watching the hand Théo was playing against himself. Then, without waiting for a reply, she moved her head slightly in the direction of the little gate at the bottom of the garden, indicating that, when coming over, she had seen two cars with young men in them, almost like an ambush, over by the neighbors' property.

I T BEGAN WITH THE NOISE OF BRANCHES down
by the river, where Michèle said she had seen the
cars. Ania got up and walked through the grass to
see what was going on. Someone appeared to be in
the process of hoisting himself up an elder tree to
climb onto the house of the artisans. Ania couldn't
see who it was, only a blur of color through the
branches, then an agile silhouette landed on the
cement roof. Almost simultaneously, there was a
noise of broken glass that led to raucous laughter
over by the cars. "Do you think they're trying to
come here?" Ania asked, turning to Michèle. "No,
they would have come by the gate; they saw me
enter a little while ago." Ania took a few more steps.
The young man on the roof had jumped back into
the trees to climb down. There was a great shaking

of foliage, then his friends could be heard laughing and the cars accelerating rapidly. Ania had moved to the middle of the field to get a better view. Smoke began to rise from the small house and she could hear the cracking of dead wood. Suddenly, the door flew open and the neighbor ran toward the river screaming "Fire!" Ania watched him pick up a rock and threw it at one of the departing automobiles. She turned around, concerned about Théo. But he was collecting his cards under the watchful eye of Michèle, who took him by the hand and led him inside. Ania watched them disappear behind the tall French windows, which Michèle closed behind her, then she moved toward the burning house.

The wind drove the smoke toward the river and the red glow of the fire could be seen throughout the house. Ania moved a little closer when, suddenly, all the windows blew out at the same time. The explosion drove her back. She was waiting for the roof to collapse and sirens could already be heard in the distance. The young men in their cars drove away rapidly, followed by the shouts of passing hikers and the owners of the neighboring properties, who had come running down the path.

Ania reached the small gate by which Michèle had cleared a passage through the thorns. The unaccustomed sound of burning covered the noise of the river's current. The fire was beginning to reach the reeds and the brush when a stream of water began to snake through the trees like a whip. None of the windows in the house remained, just two gaping rectangles and, behind, a cauldron of flames through which a steady rain of charred debris fell as if in slow motion. The heat was unbearable. The handful of people who had run up pulled back along the path. Closest to the inferno, the man with the red hair cast an incredulous glance from time to time. Surprised in her nightgown by the fire, his wife tried to open the door of the light green van, where the fire was also burning. A few seconds more and they would have nothing. It was the shock alone that seemed to prevent them from giving in completely to despair.

Ania stood there, staring. She was unable to

believe that this couple had had anything to do with the desecration of the grave. Nor could she comprehend the depth of resentment that had given those young men, who had been so cowardly, so hesitant to approach them yesterday, the energy for an act of such violence.

ACKNOWLEDGMENTS

I would like to thank the residents and staff of the Ancien Carmel de Condom for their warm welcome and generosity.

BELLEVUE LITERARY PRESS is devoted to publishing
literary fiction and nonfiction at the intersection of
the arts and sciences because we believe that science
and the humanities are natural companions
for understanding the human experience.
With each book we publish, our goal is to foster a
rich, interdisciplinary dialogue that will forge new
tools for thinking and engaging with the world.

To support our press and its mission,
and for our full catalogue of published titles,
please visit us at blpress.org.

BELLEVUE LITERARY PRESS
New York